COURT OF CRIMSON

TWISTED FAE
BOOK ONE

LUCINDA DARK

HELEN SCOTT

Copyright © 2023 by Lucinda Dark (Lucy Smoke LLC) & Helen Scott

All rights reserved.

No part of this book may be reproduced in any form or by any electronic or mechanical means, including information storage and retrieval systems, without written permission from the author, except for the use of brief quotations in a book review.

CONTENTS

1.	Cress	1
2.	Cress	8
3.	Cress	19
4.	Cress	26
5.	Roan	41
6.	Cress	46
7.	Cress	58
8.	Cress	67
9.	Roan	75
10.	Cress	81
11.	Orion	92
12.	Cress	101
13.	Sorrell	118
14.	Roan	125
15.	Cress	129
16.	Cress	146
17.	Cress	152
18.	Cress	157
19.	Roan	167
20.	Cress	171
21.	Cress	176
22.	Roan	190
23.	Cress	198
24.	Cress	208
25.	Cress	216
26.	Sorrell	232
27.	Cress	239
28.	Cress	246
29.	Cress	257

About Lucinda Dark	267
Also by Lucinda Dark	269
About Helen Scott	273
Also by Helen Scott	275

Copyright © 2020 by Lucinda Dark & Helen Scott

All rights reserved. Lucy Smoke LLC & Helen Scott

No part of this book may be reproduced in any form or by any electronic or mechanical means, including information storage and retrieval systems, without written permission from the author, except for the use of brief quotations in a book review.

Cover Design by Covers by Christian

Editing by Your Editing Lounge & Ms. Correct All's Editing

Proofreading by Ellen Yates

Chapter 1
CRESS

My stomach rumbled again as I quietly shut the door to the Abbess' office. That was a big fat waste of my time. I took a quick peek behind me and once I was secure that the coast was clear that way, I turned and headed for the kitchen. Maybe I'd be able to hoard a few extra days of rationings for the journey I'd have before me at the very least. Mmmmm ... I loved bread.

Upon my first step down into the room that smells of the fresh baked slices of God heaven, I knew that plan was going to be dashed all to hell. "Aha! I knew you were bound to come searching for food after this morning." Sister Madeline's proud scoffing sounded far more like an enraged baker's wife than a kind nun. I froze with my foot on the stone floor and blinked like a deer caught at the wrong end of someone's bow and arrow just before the arrow was released. Sister Madeline came huffing and puffing around the corner and snatched up my wrist before I had a chance to escape. "I'm taking you to Mother Collette as soon as service ends," she hissed, tightening her grip as her dull brown eyes narrowed on my face. "You'll get what's coming to you—first for your insolence this morning then for sneaking in here and trying to steal food."

"I—I—" There was no use in trying to deny it. Her wickedly sharp nails bit into the flesh of my wrist, tightening until I was sure she would break the skin.

"I caught you, little thief," she hissed into my face, spittle flying from her dry, cracked lips and hitting me in the face as she towered over me in her dark nun garb, "and I'll make sure you're punished this time."

My lips turned down as she hauled me out of the kitchen, dragging me behind her. There was no doubt in my mind she would. Sister Madeline was perhaps the most violent nun I'd ever met, and I couldn't count the number of times she'd been all too happy to wallop me on my ass or across my knuckles for even the smallest transgression. Though there was nothing in my hands to proclaim me caught red-handed, missing evening service was good enough for a serious ass whipping.

Letting out a breath, I cursed myself for not being more observant. I must have missed her returning to the kitchen while I was in the Abbess' office. At the very least, though, she hadn't caught me there. I didn't want to think what would've happened had I been caught trying to pilfer money rather than an extra loaf of bread.

∽

Hours and one burning backside later, I crawled onto my cot next to Nellie's well after evening service had ended and released a deep groan. My belly continued to cramp with its emptiness, but that was the least of my concerns. I laid out on my stomach to avoid any more touching of my back and ass. Mother Catherine hadn't gone easy. She never did. I buried my face into the stiff, straw pillow in front of me and forced back the scream of frustration.

"Hey," Nellie's soft voice reached my ears, "are you awake?"

I lifted my head and blew a strand of white-blonde hair out of my eyes. "What do you think?" I grumbled.

After a beat, she replied, "You're right, that was a dumb question."

When she didn't say anything more and the silence began to beat at me harder than Mother Catherine's thrashing, I groaned again and looked her way. Nellie had her thin sheet pulled up over her tiny frame. Her small fingers tightened around the edge of the blanket, her knuckles white with strain. "What?" I asked.

"I know you don't like it here," she whispered, "but do you think you could try to get along with everything. I don't want ... I don't want them to throw you out."

"Throw me out?" I scoffed. "Nel, my birthday's in two days. As soon as I hit the big two-one, I'm out of here."

"What?" Nellie sat up abruptly, squeaking out the word, and somewhere in the room, one of the other girls grumbled in their sleep.

I blew out a breath. "What did you think would happen?" I asked. "Twenty-one is when you leave. Doesn't matter what I do."

"But I-I thought you were gonna take the vows," she said. "I'm going to take them."

I snorted. "Why the hell would I do that?" I asked. That was the most ridiculous thing I'd ever heard. "Listen, Nel," I slowly pushed myself up from the bed and edged over onto my side so I could see her better, "I was dropped here at three months old. I've lived in Amnestia all my life, and for me, this place is a prison. I don't fit in and I never have. Like Sister Madeline always says, I'm too wild a creature to ever belong with civilized people." And if wild was code for fun, then I didn't mind being wild. Sister Madeline was as staid as an old cow.

"She was upset when she said that," Nellie defended.

I chuckled as I raised one brow. "She's upset with me a lot then. She hates me."

"Only because you provoke her," Nellie snapped, squeezing her blanket in her fists. One of the girls, who wasn't yet asleep, shushed us from several rows down. Nellie winced and laid back down, pulling her sheet up to her chin. "If you didn't provoke the sisters so much, everything would be fine."

"Whether I provoke them or not, Nel, I just don't

belong here. Besides ... there's something I have to find."

"What is it?" she asked, turning her head curiously.

I pressed my lips together and rolled back onto my front, folding my arms under my head. "Just ... something," I hedged. I didn't want to tell her that just like the rest of the orphans here, I wanted to find out where I came from. Deep down, it was more than a desire—it was a need. I had to find out why I'd been left here twenty-one years ago.

Nellie watched me for a moment more before shaking her head. "It's dangerous out there. You don't know it because you've never left the abbey before—or well, not past the village—but there are things out in the wild—creatures of magic and lore. I've seen them with my own eyes."

My eyes snapped to the side. "What? Really? Why haven't you ever said anything? What were they like?" I asked, edging closer to her excitedly. I'd only heard brief mentions of the creatures the King and his knights fought with on the southern battlefields. Never before had I heard of anyone who'd actually seen them. "What did you see?"

Nellie's eyes found the ceiling overhead and she stared at it unblinkingly. "My parents were doctors," she whispered. "Did I ever tell you that?"

I shook my head, frowning. *What did that have to do with Fae?* I thought. "Uh ... no?"

"They were," she nodded as if affirming that fact. "They were doctors on one of the battlefields in the southern quarter. And because we didn't have any other family, they took me with them. I helped bring bandages and take care of the men who..." She drifted off, her breath catching as her fingers tightened even further on the sheets tugged up to her chest. "We weren't in the middle of the action—that's why they thought it would be okay—but we were on the edge. The soldiers should've known better. The creatures they were fighting—I saw one. It was big, as big as a dragon but without the scales. It had wings of the finest feathers like a shower of autumn leaves. And riding upon it was something far more magnificent."

I sat up and scooted as close to the corner of my bed as I could. "What was it?"

"It was a Faerie," she whispered, her voice catching and lowering as if just the word itself might make one appear out of thin air.

"A Faerie," I repeated the word, letting the syllables dangle on my tongue. It felt like such a strange word on my lips, and yet at the same time, it felt familiar.

"They're otherworldly," she confessed. "Beautiful and savage. It was that Faerie and whatever the creature it rode upon that destroyed the entire human base my parents lived in. It only took one. The magic he possessed—it was so strong and it rained down in a wave of fire. I'd been running a message to someone else," she said. "I was spared. But sometimes I wonder what would have happened had I been in the camp with everyone else. Would I have felt pain? Did my parents...?"

Her eyes were foggy, clouded over by the images of her past and guilt ate away at my insides, curdling like spoiled milk in my stomach. I shouldn't have pushed her to relay the memories. They were obviously painful and terrifying for her.

"It's okay. You don't have to tell me anything else," I promised. "That's enough."

Nellie sucked in a shaky breath and turned to look at me. "When you leave, no matter what you do," she said, "don't go south. They're dangerous. Faeries may look like fallen Gods, but they're much worse. They're death incarnate and they destroy everything they touch."

I nodded and despite the pain in my back and ass, I reached over and patted her hand. "Okay," I said. "It'll be okay. You're safe here."

She closed her eyes and turned away, but not before I saw the single crystalline tear that slid from her closed eye down her cheek. To Nellie—and others like her—Faeries meant danger. It was what we humans feared. It was what our King and his knights battled against. But me ... I felt something else—something that had gotten me into trouble far more often than not.

Curiosity.

CHAPTER 2
CRESS

A yawn stretched my mouth as I lounged back on the sun warmed stone rooftop. Even at the depths of twilight, when the air was growing colder, the feel of the dying sunshine on my face lulled me into a listless half-asleep state. Sleeping, after all, was the best past time to have. Not that the nuns of the Abbey of Amnestia would necessarily agree with me, but they didn't know where I was, so I didn't have to listen to their scolding and I could nap in peace. It was only the ricocheting clanking sounds of someone climbing up the creaky old half-rusted ladder I'd stashed on the side of the storehouse that drew me out of my dreamy state. I peeked one eyelid open as a petite form appeared over the side of the stone roof—wispy strawberry blonde hair flitting in the semi-cool breeze. I sighed.

"Sister Lena is going to be so mad at me if she finds out the reason you're missing is because you came looking for me again," I commented lightly as Nellie finished clambering onto the slanted rooftop.

"Sister—*ugh!*" Nellie grunted as she gripped the edge of the roof and shimmied up and over the last rung of the ladder where there was still a two foot difference from that to the roof. "Lena," she continued once she was stable, "wouldn't have anything to worry about if you'd stop coming up here."

Nellie crawled across the space left until she made it to my side. I let my eye slide shut again now that I knew she was safe. She may only be a year or two younger than me but there was something fragile about her, something that was far too delicate to be climbing up onto rooftops—not that I was much taller—but let's be honest, I was far more adept at not killing myself. Most of the time, anyway. Minor bruises, some fractured bones, and lacerations were not cause for concern when it came to me. Just the norm. The sisters liked to say that I was prone to accidents. I liked to say that accidents were prone to me. "Where else am I going to find a place to nap? If I try to stay in my bed, Sister Madeline finds me and makes me work in the stables."

"You're just lazy," Nellie snapped. "Maybe if you did your work, Sister Madeline wouldn't have to chastise you so much." I didn't have to see it to know that Nellie had both of her fists planted on her hips as she sat on her knees and glared down at me. Sister Lena did that same thing when she was pushed past her breaking point, and Nellie followed that woman around like she was her little duckling.

I grinned without opening my eyes, the feel of it stretching my cheeks. "She can chastise all she wants," I replied. "It won't suddenly turn me into her favorite person." I re-cracked the same eye. "Or make me not want to nap. Napping is the best." I closed my eye again.

Nellie huffed out a breath and a moment later, I felt her petite form thump beside me as her arm brushed my side. "Heard you refused to eat again today," she said quietly, making me stiffen.

"I didn't refuse," I said, pouting petulantly. "I just … told them I wasn't hungry."

"Did you tell them you weren't hungry after calling them murderers and dumping a plate of ham on someone's head?"

I grimaced and then snorted. I *had* done that, but only after the sisters in charge of feeding us orphans had called me an ungrateful leech who was too lazy and stupid to survive if it weren't for their goodwill. I wasn't ungrateful for everything they did, but I couldn't stomach some of the things that made their way across the table—specifically if said things had previously had a face. And since we were surrounded by farmland, a lot of faces made it across our table—pigs, cows, chickens, and even wild boar. But the meat, for some reason, always made me sick.

"You can't call what they were trying to serve ham," I replied tartly, opening my eyes. "It was burnt to a crisp and smelled of oil. I was pretty sure they just stuck some mold and meat together and tried to burn it so no one would notice."

"And if it hadn't been burnt?" Nellie pressed. "If it was just ham, would you have eaten it?" When I didn't answer, she sighed. "I don't know what to do with you, Cress." She shook her head forlornly. "You have to eat."

"I *do* eat," I reminded her, staring up as a cloud drifted in front of the sun.

"Usually when kids refuse to eat, it's their vegetables they're not interested in. That's *all* you eat. It's probably why you're so short."

I sat up and turned, casting her a dark glare. "I am *not* short," I snapped. I was a perfectly acceptable height for my age. I was taller than Nellie, for sure ... sometimes ... when she didn't stand up straight or get on her tip toes. I scowled. "You're not one to talk. You're a whole two inches shorter. I'm still the taller one of us both."

"I'm seventeen," she deadpanned. "I'm still growing. You're twenty—almost twenty-one."

I groaned and flopped back against the roof. She had a point. "I don't know why I can't eat it," I admitted quietly. "I've tried before—it just made my stomach hurt really bad for days. Sister Lena thought I was gonna die."

"Pretty sure Sister Madeline would've liked that," Nellie muttered.

I laughed. "Yeah, you're probably right. She hates me."

Nellie looked at me, her soft brown eyes beseeching. "Just come down and do your chores and eat, won't you? Be nice to the sisters and when the Abbess gets back from her trip, maybe they won't mention everything."

I snorted at that. "They always mention it, doesn't matter what I do."

I turned my head and looked out over the vast countryside. Sheep and cows munched on dry grass in the near distance. Little hut houses dotted the land, most of them in a collection not far from our little convent. I glanced down and picked at a piece of fringe from the frayed hem on my uniform shirt—it was just like the one Nellie wore. The nuns had taken us in—some as babies like I'd been and some as older children, like Nellie—but none of us were unique in their eyes. We were just mouths to feed. Every year, more and more arrived after losing their parents in the southern wars with the Fae.

Across the small courtyard of the abbey's land, church bells for evening service rang. Nellie sat up abruptly. "Oh shoot," she said. "We're late."

"You can make it if you shimmy down and cut through the kitchens," I said absently as I settled back against the stones.

"Aren't you coming?" she asked as she crawled back across the roof towards where the ladder was.

I shook my head and let my eyes slide shut as the sun began to set over the horizon. "Nah, I don't think so," I said. "I'd rather take another nap."

She scoffed. "If they catch you sneaking in after missing evening services, they're going to thrash you."

"That's *if* they catch me," I replied, opening my eyes and shooting her a grin as she slipped over the side of the roof.

When just the top half of her face was visible, she narrowed her gaze on me and huffed. "Fine," she snapped. "Suit yourself. It's *your* hide that's gonna be reddened before the day is through."

I shrugged, which only served to irritate her more and true to her age, she rolled her eyes at me before disappearing altogether, leaving me to relish in the last remaining rays of sunlight as the big glowing red ball of heat slipped behind the mountain range. I didn't understand it, but feeling the sun on my skin—even as far from it as it felt like our little backwoods rural community was—made me feel energized. I'd lied when I said I was going to take a nap. The truth was that I'd been waiting for the evening service all day. Every day, like clockwork, the nuns—or brides of Coreliath as some referred to them—would gather the rest of the orphans and preach about the feats of the God King they spent their lives worshipping, forgoing all physical pleasures and remaining chaste in the hopes that he would pluck the most virtuous of them to live with him in the afterlife.

While they were absorbed in their prayers, however, I had to think about the real world. Sure, Gods might've been real once—long ago—but now we had more tangible monsters to concern ourselves with.

Like starvation and homelessness. In two days' time, it would be my twenty-first birthday and that meant that in less than forty-eight hours, I'd be exiled from the Abbey of Amnestia unless I took the vows of chastity required of the Brides of Coreliath. I laughed internally at that thought.

Yeah, fat chance of that happening. I didn't want to remain a virgin for the rest of my life. I *wanted* them to exile me. I needed to leave these walls. The sooner I did, the better. Who wanted to be stuck on the same little patch of land for their entire lives? Certainly not me. I was getting out even if it killed me. Which it might. Hopefully not. But I mean ... there was always a chance. What with dangerous Faeries and all sorts of other creatures crawling over the countryside, and I'd been known to trip over nothing but air a time or two.

It was a blessing that our little rural community was as far from the war as possible. When I was kicked out, at least I wouldn't have to worry about running headfirst into a battlefield. Knowing my luck, I'd somehow find a way. I swore, if I didn't know any better, I'd think I was cursed by Coreliath—but why would he give a shit about a nobody like me? Answer: he didn't. Thank the Gods. But that left me with one understanding—I was the one responsible for all of my mishaps and accidents. Clumsy, thy name is Cressida.

Still, my impending expatriation from the abbey brought with it other ... issues. If I was gonna be homeless for the foreseeable future, I'd need far more than the scraps they were likely to give me—barely enough for a three day journey. I'd need money to get, well, basically anywhere.

I sat up as the church bells rang into silence and the sound of the church's large door echoed up the stone building's exterior walls as it was slammed shut. It was time to execute plan A.

I slipped down the ladder and headed for the convent's main building. It housed the nuns' sleeping quarters, but more than that, it housed the Abbess' office—the head honcho, the big cheese, the end all be all of the sister's lives—other than their imagined God husband. The Abbess was rarely ever there—since she chose to traverse the countryside for some ridiculous reason or another—spreading charity or love or whatever Abbesses did. A horse whinnied at me as I passed through the stables and I lifted a palm with a smile, pressing a finger to my lips with a wink.

"Shhh, Isabelle," I whispered. "You don't want to get me caught, do you?"

I shook my head with a small smile as if the horse could understand me, but she quieted nonetheless, stomping her feet in her hay before she turned her head and whipped a bit of her mane into my face. Rude horse. I chuckled anyway, flicking her dark horsehair out of my face. "Sassy girl," I chastised, reaching through her stall to give her a gentle pat before I continued on my way.

I peeked into the empty courtyard, darting my gaze left and then right before I left the safety of the stables and raced up the front steps and into the building. I had to go faster, move quicker—before anyone thought to leave the church. Before the chance was gone. The Abbess' office was in the back—next to the kitchens and the nuns' sleeping quarters. I hurried for it, pausing when I thought I heard someone beyond the kitchen doorway.

Sweat coated the back of my neck, making the white-blonde strands of my hair stick to me. I gulped back a breath, reaching for the doorknob, turning it, and moving at the same time as a footstep creaked on the wood flooring several paces down the hallway. I eased the door shut behind me and pressed my back to the door, panting with relief when a woman's voice—Sister Madeline's, I realized—sounded from beyond the door. A few seconds more and the mean, old coot would've caught me.

"Stupid girl, of course she's not here. Where the hell could she be? Missing evening service after all that she's been given. Ungrateful little—" I breathed a sigh of relief when her voice faded off down the hall. She'd been in the building looking for me. That wasn't surprising. Her vitriol didn't surprise me either. From Sister Madeline, it'd always been 'you're such a lazabout' this or 'can't you do anything right?' that. I could certainly do things right. I could hold my breath underwater for two and a half minutes. According to Nellie, that was an accomplishment and I'd take those when I could get them.

I let my head sink back on my shoulders as I stared up at the ceiling. My heart thundered in my ears, and it took several moments of even breaths to calm it. Once I had it under control, I looked back to the rest of the room. A large oak wood desk with a plush cushioned chair behind it. Velvet drapes lined the window even further back and twin floor-to-ceiling wooden shelves lined the walls. I whistled quietly as I tiptoed further into the space. I'd never been called to the Abbess' office before, and to my knowledge, none of the other orphans had either. I wondered what Nellie would do if she knew that the Abbess was living large while we were all scraping to survive.

Ducking behind the desk, I rummaged through the drawers. Papers. Ink quills. More papers. Seals. But no purse. No money. No coins. No nothing! I grew frustrated the longer I searched, clenching my hands into fists as I huffed and snarled, digging through what was left in the drawers. But of course, I still found nothing more than dust and more parchment. My stomach rumbled, reminding me that I'd refused to eat the stuff they'd called food earlier. Hunger made me that much crankier.

Slamming the last drawer shut with a curse, I gave up on searching the Abbess' office. *I should've known better*, I thought as I headed back into the hallway. What with the wars down south and the famine from last year's harvest, the nuns weren't likely to have just any extra coins lying about. It was a ridiculous notion to begin with, one born of panic at my nearing homelessness. My strings would be cut, and I'd be left with nothing but the clothes on my back—going back into the world practically as I'd come into it. I mean there were worse things, right? I had my looks, but I'd heard about what happened to pretty young girls who didn't have anywhere to go, and I had absolutely no intention of being a kept woman. Maybe. Probably not. But then, what did being a kept woman even mean?

As I thought about it, I did hear that they, at least, got to sleep in. Maybe that wouldn't be so bad. I'd always preferred to sleep in than get up at the asscrack of dawn like the nuns required us to.

CHAPTER 3
CRESS

I slept fitfully that night. My ass and back were covered in red welts, but that wasn't the reason. My dreams, or rather my nightmares, kept me tossing and turning. I never had nightmares like this. But even in my half-awake state, I could sense that something was different. My insides churned with agony and a violent pitchy noise scratched at the back of my head. I didn't know when it had started, only that it wasn't gone by the time the sun was beginning to lighten the sky outside of our windows. At first, I thought it was a clanging—like someone was banging pots and pans nearby—but then by the time the bells rang in the morning to rouse the others, it was more of a whistling or whooshing sound as though something was moving faster and faster every second that ticked by.

I groaned as I forced myself to get up, pressing a hand to my temple. With the state my back and ass were in, I couldn't afford to get another whipping today, not unless I wanted to be scarred for life. Sister Madeline had made sure no one went easy on me. I was sore from my top to my bottom—quite literally.

Everyone else was already gone from their bunks, doing their chores no doubt, like good little girls and boys. I, on the other hand, was not going to do that. I had other plans for the day and none of them involved doing my chores. Not that any of the sisters expected me to do my chores anymore—they'd gotten used to my "laziness" as they called it. Whereas I preferred to call it conserving my energy.

Less than two days until I would be booted from the convent and the time seemed to be streaking by. That was fine by me, there was a big world out there to see and I wanted to see it all, especially if I managed to find what I was looking for. The only problem that still presented itself to me was that if I was going to see it all then I needed money to do so—money to travel, to pay for room and board, or just food. If I didn't have something figured out before they kicked me out then I'd be homeless and penniless and whatever scraps they fed me before effectively closing the gates on my ass weren't going to last me very long.

The loud noise I'd been hearing screeched throughout the room. I had to cover my ears to try and protect them from the awful noise as it reverberated off the stone walls. I hurried to wash and dress so I could get downstairs and find out what the hell was going on. Had the war made its way north? Was a battle coming to the grounds of Amnestia? We hadn't heard anything from the local village.

Thoughts and questions bounced around my mind as I hurried to get ready. My feet slapped the stone steps, my shoes barely hanging onto them as I rushed downstairs, only to find everyone acting as though nothing was happening—as if that whistling, rushing noise wasn't ringing through the air.

"Don't you fucking hear that?" I practically yelled to one of the cooks as I barreled through the kitchen. I was almost completely out of the kitchen and into the gravel area between the main building and the barns when Sister Ermine's quiet response registered in my frazzled brain.

"Watch your mouth!" she snapped before frowning at me and moving my way. "And what the blazes are you talking about? Hear what?"

I clamped my hands over my ears once more and turned to find everyone that was working in the kitchen staring through the open door, gaping at me like I was going mad. Maybe I was. Only one way to find out.

"Can you really not hear it?" I yelled over the sound. "That infernal noise!"

A few of the kitchen staff jumped at my words before rushing back to what they were doing, as though whatever was going on with me was catching. They had to be playing a joke on me, surely? The sisters weren't known for their sense of humor but there was a first time for everything.

I turned, looking for the source of the sound, but there were no clues as to what it was or where it was coming from. My inability to find the source of the noise made it almost more painful. It was like I was standing inside one of the large bells at the top of the church while someone repeatedly hit it with a giant stick. The force of it was enough to vibrate through my whole body and left me on my knees in the dirt as I panted and tried, unsuccessfully, to block it from my mind.

Sister Madeline was there the next instant, the sneer on her lips enough to tell me I'd find no sympathy from her, not that I'd expected any. I avoided her, unable to hear her when she started talking. The noise grew louder, banging around inside my skull. I squinted and felt tears start to leak down my cheeks. Gods, it hurt so fucking badly. *Would it ever stop?* I wondered. *Would I have to live the rest of my life, shouting over the sound in my head, crying at the pain?* I collapsed against a wall with a horrible sob.

It was when Nellie's worried face appeared in front of mine, her mouth creased into a frown as she squinted at me, that I actually started to panic. Her lips moved, but I couldn't hear her voice anymore, all I could hear was the high-pitched spinning racket as it spiraled through my head.

I couldn't feel the hands moving over me, but soon enough someone must have called for the nurse's stretcher. The noise was so debilitating that it was all I could do to force more tears back as I was rolled onto it. Even my groan didn't make it to my ears, I only knew I'd made the noise from the rise of my chest and the reverberation as I parted my dry lips. Nothing good ever came from being on the stretcher. It meant a visit to see Sister Christine, and she didn't tolerate fools or pranks. The bed in her office was about as old as the rickety stretcher I curled up on. I squeezed my eyes shut as whoever it was that had been called to carry me—likely a couple of the older orphan boys—hefted me up from the ground. The stretcher's middle sagged under my weight, and I was nearly dropped back onto the cold hard gravel. I was worried the old fabric and wood wouldn't be able to hold me, but I couldn't even speak to tell them to stop trying.

Sharp spikes of pain lanced through me. Something cool and wet leaked from my ears. My eyes popped open and I reached up to touch the liquid. When I pulled my hands away, a red sheen of blood covered my fingertips nearly making my heart stop. I looked up. They had to see this. I wasn't making it up. Sister Madeline was standing alongside the stretcher and there was no doubt in my mind that she saw. Her eyes were focused on my fingers, her expression morphing from a sneer of contempt to actual concern. She lifted her head to the ones holding me.

"Hurry," she snapped—her voice coming through muffled and warped around the noise still screeching through my eardrums. "Get her to Sister Christine." To have this woman—the one who'd hated me for years

—act out of genuine worry only made me panic even more.

If she was being nice to me, then I was almost certainly dying.

By the time we got to Sister Christine's office, the noise had grown so impossible, I was clenching my teeth and forcing back screams. I parted my lips as breathy pants escaped. I wanted to slam my head into the stone floor—anything that would end this torture. No matter how I tried to plug my ears, I couldn't stop the shrill loudness of it as it drilled into my head one pound of my heart at a time. Sister Christine rushed to direct the boys who carried me to the single bed she kept in the nurse's quarters. Her cool hands were on me then, trying to hold me down even while she looked me over. I couldn't stand it. I threw her off, rolling over and nearly sliding off the bed as I tried to get away. Her touch was too much. The volume of sound in my head was enough. I couldn't stand more of it as she began talking, trying to calm me.

"Stop it," I rasped out through gritted teeth. "Please, fucking stop it!" Someone said something but it was lost to the noise.

My arms were yanked away from my body as I was promptly repositioned on the bed and then my head was tilted back and cool liquid filled my mouth. I coughed, wheezing when someone held my head still as the fluid slid to the back of my throat and down into my belly. I struggled, but there were multiple hands on me—holding me steady, massaging my neck to make the liquid go down faster. No sooner had I been released than I began to feel the liquid's effects. I wavered and slumped back into the bed as sleep—no, not sleep, unconsciousness filled my mind.

They'd drugged me. Without my consent. Irritation flared bright and I clenched my nails against my palms, wishing I could get up and punch the daylights out of someone, but my limbs were lax. I was lethargic. Perhaps they'd drugged me so that they could try to figure out what was going on, but they still hadn't fucking asked. I tried to fight against the oblivion as it overtook me. I wanted to keep fighting them, but whatever herbs the nurse had mixed into the liquid were potent. They clouded my thoughts and soon enough, I didn't feel or hear anything at all.

Oh, well, this wasn't as bad as I thought, I conceded murkily just as my mind winked out like a dying star disappearing from the sky.

CHAPTER 4
CRESS

When I awoke, it was like the whole world had gone silent. I lay there for several moments, wondering if it was a trick. Or Gods—what if I was deaf? All that noise and now, nothing? It was eerie, to say the least. My head was pounding and my mouth felt like it was made of the same material as the nuns' habits, but dirtier—not the pristine black that they normally wore. I smacked my lips a few times, swiping my tongue over my teeth feeling a gritty film over them as I turned my head and took in my surroundings. As soon as my eyes lit on the glass of water sitting by the bed, I forgot my earlier fear of being deaf and lunged for it—downing it like a dehydrated man dragged out of the desert as I tried to wash the grimy sensations away.

The cool water slipped over my lips and tongue, bringing relief with it. Once the glass was emptied and my mouth didn't feel fuzzy or gritty anymore, I pushed myself up and looked around. It was night outside, that much was clear. Not even a single candle had been left lit. Darkness blanketed the room, and for some reason, it soothed my raw nerves.

On a table in the corner of the nurse's office, there was a small clock. I squinted at it, barely able to make out the time using the moon's rays as they shone in through the single window. Midnight. I sighed. It was officially my birthday, or at least what the nun's thought was my birthday.

Sliding the sheets that covered me to the side, I hopped off the bed. The cool night air flowed in through the window like a stream. I paused and lifted my head a bit, sniffing lightly. A scent hovered on the wind. It was like none I'd ever smelled. *Huh,* I wondered. *If I was deaf now, did that mean my other senses would get stronger to compensate? Wouldn't I have heard it when I set the glass back down?* I turned my head, looking at it on the bedside table. I hadn't even been paying attention. *What if I really was deaf?!* When I heard the first of the insect noises, however, as I leaned forward, that idea was thrown out the window. *Guess not,* I decided.

My heart lurched in my chest and my stomach growled with hunger. I shouldn't have been surprised by the rumbling. If it was nighttime and only a day had passed then that meant I hadn't eaten in over a day. But this hunger was different than any I'd felt before. It slithered bone deep—no, deeper. It went to the very core of my being, calling to me and forcing me to follow it. That scent leading the way as I got out of bed and headed for the door.

At first, I wasn't even paying attention to where the smell was coming from, I just followed it. Rocks and dirt and leaves crunched under my feet and I paused, the sound carrying with it a memory. I wasn't supposed to leave the grounds of the abbey without permission. My legs paused even as my body vibrated with the need to keep going. I weighed what I was supposed to do against my curiosity. It was only a moment, but at least I did it. I patted my mental self on the back even as I grinned, knowing full well what the outcome would be. I lifted my foot and kept going until my legs carried me onto the grass beyond the edge of the convent and further.

Invisible limbs grasped me as wind blew past my face, lifting the light strands of my hair and slapping my cheeks. It almost knocked me back, or it would have had those invisible grips not held me steady and firm against it. That scent refilled my nostrils. It was so strange—first the noise and now this scent. My fingers trembled as I lifted them to my face, touching my nose.

The forest beyond the convent was dark. The dark stretches of branches created a veritable ceiling of leaves that hid almost all of the moon's light from me. I felt my way blindly through the greenery, pulled by some invisible force. Those limbs that had once held me now pushed me forward. Faster and faster my legs pumped. I followed the trail I couldn't see until I came out on the other side of the treeline, stopping cold.

My lips parted, my mouth gaping as I looked up and up some more. Stone. Stacked as high as my eyes could see, nearly blocking out the mountain range behind it. I glanced back over my shoulder, through the dark forest. I'd never gone this far from the convent—at least not on this side since the local village was in the other direction, but I was sure I would've heard of this ... castle.

Castles didn't just appear out of thin air ... did they? Why had the nuns never said anything? Never mentioned it? It was crazy, absolutely insane, to say the least. I had no idea what had happened. What could make something that looked like a castle big enough to house an entire Court of people suddenly appear? Was I hallucinating? Was it some trick of the light, or lack thereof? I turned in a circle. Nope. I was still on the hillside of Amnestia. I hadn't been magically transported in my sleep. But the same couldn't be said for this monstrosity.

I froze as a thought suddenly occurred. Even when standing still, the body still moves somewhat. The chest pumps up and down as you breathe. You sway—even unintentionally—as the wind brushes against you or as you try to keep your footing. But I just ... stopped. Breathing. Moving. Swaying. Anything. Everything. As one looming question forced its way to the forefront of my mind.

Was I dead? If so, that would really suck.

I stood there, staring up at the castle for a moment more before I decided to keep going. I wasn't going to find the answers to my questions if I just stood there frozen like that. Sliding closer to the line of trees, I felt along in the semi-darkness as I began to circle the tall structure. The castle was huge—taller than the trees—with a giant wall surrounding it.

How a structure of that size and approximate age, going by the wear on the stones, as well as the complexity of its build could suddenly appear was beyond me, but it was here and it was where the smell seemed to originate from. I lifted my head and sniffed again. Sure enough, that delicious scent was emanating from somewhere beyond the wall—slightly sweet and titillating. It was almost hypnotic in its all consuming power to make me trail after it.

Even as my body leaned forward, enticed by the smell, my eyes gobbled up the sight of the castle. For the last twenty years, all I'd ever laid eyes on was the bland countryside of the convent, some cows, and chickens. Maybe some travelers, if I was lucky, not that they ever came close enough to talk to. Even the convent itself was plain. The pale cream walls covered the two levels of the building which was topped with terra-cotta tiles, save for the flat stone area of the roof over the storage house where I liked to bathe in the sun. The only other buildings were the barns and chicken coops. All of which I'd been through more than a dozen times.

This building, though, was different in so many ways. Spires shot so high into the sky that it looked as if they were touching the clouds. Thin bridges that looked like they could collapse with a strong breeze went between the spires and others seemed to roll down to the ground like great staircases. There were so many points going up into the sky that it was easy to miss the biggest one at first. It sat in the middle of the others, pointing heavenward, patiently waiting for the viewer to notice its majesty. Some kind of metal reflected the moonlight off the ridges of the spires and seemed to wink at me, daring me to come closer still.

Something shuddered through the air, filling my chest. The vibrations didn't just ripple through my skin, but deeper—somewhere in my heart—as though I was being pulled towards several directions at once. It forced me to slow my pace, but I couldn't quite bring myself to turn back to the safety of the convent. What lay in front of me felt too important, too ... magical.

Nellie's story came to mind, nearly stopping me completely in my tracks. Danger lay ahead. The unknown. But hadn't that been what I'd said I wanted just yesterday? I wanted to escape, to go somewhere else. Well, here was my desire come true. Be careful what you wish for and all that. Whatever it was beyond this wall was far too interesting for me to pass up. I'd never seen real magic. This might be my only chance. *Was this mysterious castle the work of the Fae?* I wondered even as I moved towards it. *Were they here to scout or slaughter? Had the war reached our small backwoods piece of the kingdom?*

I bit down on my lip hard as my legs kept going. Maybe it was the fact that this was the first fascinating thing to happen in ... well ... *ever*, but I couldn't help myself. I had to know. I couldn't *not* find out what was in there. Maybe this was all some insanely vivid dream thanks to the herbal tonic the nuns had forced down my throat, but I didn't feel drugged or impaired. I grimaced and reached up to scratch my jaw. That wasn't to say that I was in my right mind—who ever was, really? Everyone back at the convent had always thought I was a bit odd. Truth be told, if they could see me now, wandering around the hillside in whatever nightdress they had put me in, looking for the entrance to a strange castle? Well, I'm sure the sisters would have plenty to say about that.

I pushed those old and tired thoughts away when I stumbled over something on the ground. A thick black vine protruded up through the dark soil; thorns as big as my hand littered its trunk like a warning label. *Beware*, it said. *Go any farther and risk your life.* I pursed my lips even as my eyes tracked it across the ground, searching for what it could be growing from, only to find that it was coming from the wall that wrapped around the strange castle that was, quite possibly, a hallucination. Maybe. Probably not. Hopefully? No, definitely, not hopefully. I wanted this thing to be real, not a dream. Real equaled adventure. Then again ... real could also mean death. Only one way to find out.

I shrugged and decided to risk it as I tried to step over the vines. I lifted my foot and moved forward only to have something prick me. I yelped and scrambled back, stopping and glaring down at the appendage. I lifted my foot again, higher this time—staring at the vine all the while. I didn't see it shift or move to block my path, but once again, I felt a prick. No matter how high I lifted my foot, it seemed like it wasn't enough. I sighed and dropped my foot. If I kept this up, I'd run the risk of flashing anyone that might be watching. Not the greatest first impression. *Hi, I've come to poke around your crazy, magical castle, here are my lady bits.* Yeah, not so much.

If I couldn't go over, then I'd go through. It was as simple as that, at least in my head. One hundred percent, a great plan. You know, in theory. In practice, it was just a smidge more complicated. The vines and thorns dragged at my legs and against the nightdress I was wearing, slicing through the thin cotton until anything past my knees was in tatters. A thorn caught my newly exposed leg and ripped into the skin. It wasn't a prick this time, but a slice. Like a knife blade being dragged down my flesh, not a protrusion on a plant.

I gasped as pain lanced through me. Biting down hard on my lower lip, I struggled not to cry out as I watched blood flow freely down my leg and puddle on the ground next to my foot. It didn't stop flowing either, continuing down like a river over the paleness of my leg. I needed to make a tourniquet out of something or at least bind it so that it would stem the flow. I tore two pieces off my already shredded nightdress and wrapped the cloth around my calf above the wound, tying it tight enough that the blood slowed. The second piece I used to cover the wound. It soaked through rather quickly, but at least I wasn't feeling the steady stream of liquid down my calf.

When I glanced at the ground to try and see how much blood I'd left behind, there was nothing there. I frowned, narrowing my eyes and dipping my head down. But there was nothing—it was like it had never happened at all. If it wasn't for the still fresh blood on my leg, I might have started to question my sanity even more.

The vines, however, did appear to back away from me as I began to move forward once more. The more my blood dripped against the ground, the farther back they shrank. *What was that about?* I wondered as I kept going. I stared at them, wanting answers but coming up with nothing. Nada. Zip. Zilch. Pain radiated down my legs as fresh blood continued to well and slip down my skin onto the ground. Maybe I had stumbled onto a path through the brambles, or maybe the plants really were moving out of my way. Maybe I had the power to control plants now! I reached my hand out and concentrated on the nearest bramble, trying to make it grow straight instead of curling in on itself, but nothing happened. Guess that was out. I pouted as I lifted my foot and stomped forward. If I was going to go crazy, the least my mind could do was give me magic powers.

When I came to the stone wall I felt alongside it. I paused as the stones heated under my palms. My eyes widened and I quickly snatched them back as they shifted all on their own—moving to form an entrance of sorts. More like a short dark hallway. I poked my head inside, but it didn't give me much other than more of that enticing scent—like berries and sugar. Tapping my fingers against my side, I huffed out a breath. I'd come this far. Might as well keep going. I shifted through the entryway and popped out on the opposite side, coming into an empty courtyard.

And the castle was right in front of me. It was even taller up close. I swallowed. Maybe this hadn't been such a good idea. I lifted my hand and chewed my thumbnail thoughtfully. If the sisters woke and found me missing, what would they think? Would they send someone after me? Probably not. They had been planning to kick me out anyway. They'd probably be grateful. And if I died before I could get back ... what would poor Nellie think? The sisters couldn't have cared less about me if they tried, but Nellie? She'd been determined to be my friend. Lonely as that position was.

Yeah, maybe it was better that I go back. I could at least just say goodbye and inform everyone about the strange magical fortress that had suddenly appeared. I nodded to myself. That was a great idea. The best one I'd had all night. I turned, intending to do just that when I realized the entryway I'd come in through was gone.

"No, no, no, no, no," I hissed through my teeth as I spread my palms along the stones, searching for the exit, but the damn thing was gone. Vanished. Into thin air. I banged my fist against the wall in irritation, wincing when I slammed it down too hard and my fingers pressed down against my thumb. I pulled back and looked down at my thumb before glaring at the wall. "Stupid magic wall."

I kicked it, nearly falling as my foot slid out from under me. I reached out and slapped my hand against the offensive structure. When I was sure I had my footing, I turned away from it and focused my attention forward. After all, apparently the wall—or perhaps the castle?—didn't want me leaving.

It was dark, but as I moved closer to the castle, I realized that the stones that made up the fortress weren't the color of normal stones. They were encased in a layer of frost—ice creeping up and down and through the edges. The reflective twinkling on the sides that I had seen from further away was the ice glinting in the moonlight. I shivered, reaching up and rubbing my palms down my bare arms. My breath appeared in front of my face as tiny white clouds puffing from my lips. The closer I got to it, the colder I became.

I forced myself to take a deep breath of the cold air, letting it fill my lungs. My nose twitched and I leaned forward, nearly pressing my face into the stones before me. I found that the scent I'd been chasing this whole time was there, it was just dampened slightly by the cold. The intensity of it in the breath I'd taken, though, was enough to rouse my hunger once more, pushing me ever onward.

The phrase 'so close, yet so far' came to mind as I

searched for a way into the castle. I just needed to get to the other side of the wall and I'd find what I was looking for—I could feel it in my bones. A door, however, eluded me. There wasn't any way inside. The ice was a barrier, coating the stone walls and even what looked like the windows higher up.

It was the most beautiful thing I'd ever seen. It took my breath away as I watched the silvery moonlight glint off all the different facets of the frost. Yet, at the same time, it was quite bothersome. I craned my head back, staring up at the top of the spires. I hadn't realized just how far back I'd leaned when I slipped, my foot shooting out from beneath me as I fell backwards, landing on my still very sensitive behind.

A shriek of frustration escaped me, and part of me expected someone from the building to come out and tell me off for trespassing. But the castle, and the ice, remained solid and impenetrable. I pushed myself back up onto my feet and took a deep breath, letting the scent that had drawn me to the building in the first place wash over me and fill my lungs before I began searching for an entrance once more.

Finally, after it felt like I'd been hobbling around the outside for ages, I saw what had to be an opening. A huge arch opened up over the ground, making it look like the building had a gaping maw ready to devour whatever came close enough. Fear skated up and down my spine making me feel the cold of the ice even more in my thin nightdress.

I took a breath to steady myself and edged under

the archway. Part of me expected a portcullis to slam down on me, but nothing did. Instead, the cold faded and the ice seemed to thaw. A large black wood door hung in the center of the wall facing the entrance as I entered the area. The planks that made up the door were broad—easily two men wide. When I tried to open it, I had to brace one foot against the wall next to it and heave with all my might.

When the blasted thing finally gave and swung open, it slapped me in the side, shoving me to the ground like a sack of potatoes. Cursing the sisters as my butt hit the rocky floor once more, I reached back and rubbed against my sore flesh. Getting to my feet for what felt like the umpteenth time, I hurried inside before the door swung shut. I just had to hope I'd be able to open it and get back out again. The thought sent a tendril of fear winding through me, but I ignored it. It was too late to turn back now.

The hallway was dark once the door clicked shut behind me, and I wasn't sure which way to go, especially because I couldn't see what lay in either direction. Sconces on the walls burst into flame, making me yelp in surprise as light bloomed down the hallway on each side.

I chuckled uncomfortably to myself. "Well, that's convenient..." *Too convenient, perhaps?*

The scent I'd been following wound its way into my nose and down to my belly, making my mouth water. It was definitely stronger on one side than the other so I followed my nose, like I had been doing all night. The further I traveled, the more sconces lit up. It was as though they could sense my presence and were responding to an unspoken request to light my way.

Eventually, after countless twists and turns, I found myself standing at a side entrance to a giant ballroom or possibly a throne room. I wasn't sure which without venturing further inside. Tables lined each side, piled high with food, all of which smelled delicious.

Hesitantly, I stepped forward, edging into the room a fraction at a time until I reached a pillar that seemed to be one of many that lined the outskirts of the massive area. Definitely a ballroom, I decided. Perhaps one that could be transformed into a throne room. The table closest to me was overflowing with rolls. Steam rose from them, like they were fresh out of the oven. It wafted my way. There was absolutely no way I could resist.

I reached out and swiped two, before disappearing back into the hallway where I greedily took a giant bite of one. The doughy mixture melted in my mouth and tasted divine. It put anything the nuns had ever made to shame and made me wonder what I'd been missing out on all my life if this was what a simple roll tasted like.

When I had finished the rolls I'd pilfered, I debated for only a split second before creeping back into the room and making my way to the table again. I grabbed another roll, but this time I also grabbed what looked like a pastry of some kind. I didn't care what it was, so long as it tasted as good as the rolls.

"Well, well, what do we have here?" A voice sounded behind me, making me freeze and drop the food I'd collected to the floor.

CHAPTER 5
ROAN

The three of us stood in a circle over the yawning opening of the Lanuaet—the giant sphere of magical energy that allowed the three of us to control the entirety of our castle, moving the monstrosity at will. Unlike most other Fae forts, however, powered by at least four Court royals, ours was only powered by three.

Across from me, Orion and Sorrell's faces were masked with pain as they held their arms up, pouring their energy into the sphere. I winced and nearly stumbled under the backlash of the weight of the magic.

"Don't you fucking dare," Orion cursed, sweat pouring down his face. "We're almost there."

"Go fuck a Gryphon," I snarled, righting my footing and shoving the magical pulsing back into the ball of energy. "I've got this."

Sorrell snorted quietly, the white-blue strands of his hair blowing against his lips as he made the sound, but he said nothing more. Not that the bastard would. No, he was as cold as the ice magic he was currently forcing into the coalition of magics that was necessary to move the fortress. My stomach churned as I forced more of my crimson power alongside his and Orion's.

We weren't going to make it, I realized soon thereafter. It was sucking too much magic from us. We were losing control. I cursed as more sweat poured down my temples and the churning pain in my gut moved up to my chest, tightening around my Fae heart. "We have to land it," I hissed.

Orion threw me a look of surprise. "We're not there yet," he said.

I shook my head. "If we don't land it, we're not going to fucking make it."

"He's right," Sorrell said. "We land it or it'll kill us."

Orion refocused on his task, the muscles of his face pulled taut as he fought against the dark hold of his power. "Where?" he barked a moment later.

It didn't matter where, I thought. But I supposed landing smack dab in the middle of a human army camp wouldn't do. I closed my eyes and opened them once more, looking into the Lanuaet and searching for a place to land this Gods forsaken castle. I felt blood slide out of my nose. "There!" I nodded to a section of land not far off from a human village, but just secluded enough for us to remain off their radar. Orion and Sorrell nodded and together, we steered our portalled Court in the direction we wanted.

After several more gut wrenching minutes of

energy, we managed to land the fortress in a remote location. As soon as the Lanuaet released us, the three of us collapsed against the floor. I lay on my back, my torso aching with each breath I dragged into my lungs.

"Gods," I swore. "Is it just me or does it get harder every time we move this blasted thing?"

Orion grunted his agreement as he got to his feet, weaving like a drunkard as he left the oratory that housed our fort's Lanuaet. I laid there for a moment more, needing the extra time to catch my breath. As soon as I had, I leveraged up and gripped the railing that overlooked the Lanuaet, glancing up at the glowing orb with a scowl. Though we were of the strongest of the Courts, controlling such a powerful spell was still an exhausting maneuver.

"I'm hungry," I grunted as I headed for the door, not looking back as Sorrell, too, got up and moved to follow me. "The pixies better have left us a feast in the throne room. I need it."

"They always do," Sorrell said simply. I turned and watched as he faded into the dark hallway of the castle, heading back to his quarters to likely rest and recuperate.

I pivoted and went the opposite way. Bath first. Then food and maybe a fuck. I scratched my jawline, going through the list of my normal bedmates. Most of them would be asleep by now—we'd taken much longer to move the fortress than usual. I scowled as I got to the bathing room. Stripping my tunic over my head and jerking the flap of my trousers open as I divested myself of the rest of my clothes, I waded into the pool of cool waters and dunked my head beneath the surface.

It took longer and longer to move this monstrosity the more we did it—sapping our strength and leaving us practically helpless for several hours afterwards. I lifted one arm from the waters and stared at my skin—practically translucent. My blood was weak now and would be until I ate and fucked.

Slumping back against the pool's underwater settee, I grumbled. My usual bedmate, Ariana, would be furious if I woke her now. I'd make it good for her, as I always did, but the whining and complaining I'd have to deal with later would be such a fucking hassle.

I finished washing up and left the pool, finding new clothes left for me by the resident cleaning pixies on a long bench just outside of the bathing chambers. Drying off and redressing, I headed for the throne room. Food first, I decided.

No sooner had I taken a step into the throne room and I saw a small little creature—a girl—dart out from one of the pillars aligning the grand hall to snatch a roll from the feast table. I paused and frowned. I didn't recognize the girl. She was thin and wispy, big eyes, and a small mouth. She looked to be hardly more than a child until she turned and I caught a full glimpse of her from the front. *No, definitely not a child*, I thought with a grin. This was a woman. Her shape was tapered, her breasts full, and though she moved like a little mouse—biting into the food meant for my stomach like it was manna from the realm of the Gods—I did find her to be quite attractive. Perhaps I wouldn't have to forgo my post-energy sapping fuck.

"Well, well," I said. "What do we have here?"

The girl froze, the pastry and roll in her hand falling to the floor. She turned in slow, tiny increments —like a puppet being pulled on a string—until she faced me, her eyes even wider now than before. That's when her scent hit me.

Human.

Just as abruptly as I'd been startled by her presence, I was more than floored by it now. How the hell had she gotten into the castle? I strode forward, inhaling a deep breath and letting it fill me up— stretching my chest.

The girl squeaked and backed up as I towered over her.

"I don't know how a *human*," I spat the name of what she was with disgust, "got into my castle, but..." I stopped when I had her up against a pillar and punched the stone above her head, making her eyes widen as she blinked up at me. "I'm going to make sure you regret coming here."

CHAPTER 6
CRESS

I'd never seen a man so ... well ... big. As big as the statue of Coreliath—the God King that the nuns worshipped—that sat at the back of the church's altar inside the Convent of Amnestia. Coreliath was only one of many Gods worshipped across the kingdom, but as the God King, he was the most popular, and right now, I felt like I was in his presence.

The man—God?—stalked forward after startling me, his face a mask of darkness—eyes boiling with anger and something more, something I wasn't quite sure how to describe. His lips—full and beautiful—curled down into a scowl as he backed me into a pillar and pinned me there with his glare.

"Human," he snapped and it took me a moment to realize he meant me. Me. *I* was the human. And if he was referring to me as human then that must have meant that he ... wasn't? "Speak."

I frowned up at him. "I'm not a dog," I replied. "You

can't just order me to speak like a well-trained mongrel."

The anger in his face didn't disappear, but it did shift, parting to allow confused shock through as his brows rose ever so slightly and his scowl slackened. I crossed my arms over my chest, noticing that the movement drew his gaze downward. Which reminded me that I was still dressed in the nightdress I'd woken up in and the lower half of it was ripped to shreds. I swallowed roughly as my skin heated under his gaze, pressing my lips together as I tried to ignore my embarrassment. I had no reason to feel embarrassed. If anyone should feel embarrassed, it was this asshole. I mean, who came upon an innocent maiden—meaning me—while she was procuring food and scared the daylights out of her. Sure, I was stealing it and probably from him, but disrupting a lady while she was eating was just plain rude.

When his eyes rose and met mine once more there was a fire glowing in their depths and a wicked grin that spread over his face. "And yet you did."

It took me a second to realize he was referring to the command to speak that he had given me. He was right. He'd demanded I speak and I did, even if it was to throw his words back in his face. I opened my mouth to respond and watched as he quirked one of the thick slashes of his eyebrows at me in challenge. My mouth snapped shut before I could get into an argument with this ... *man*. I scowled.

"Oh, come now, human, where did all that fire go

so quickly?" he asked with a dark chuckle. A shiver chased up my spine at the low tone of his voice. Goosebumps rose down the lengths of my arms as images of scandalous things infiltrated my mind at the sound. When I stubbornly refused to respond, the chuckle deepened. "You're going to regret breaking into my castle. I assure you. I want to know how you came to find this place, how you managed to sneak inside without tripping any of our alarms, and I want to know if there are more of you."

Before I could react or open my mouth to ask what he was talking about, he turned and strode across the room, back to the entrance.

"Get her cleaned up," he called out to the seemingly empty air before turning an eye back on me. "She reeks of humans," he finished with an indelicate curl of his upper lip. My lips popped open. I did not reek! ... Did I? As discreetly as possible, I tilted my head down and to the side trying to smell myself. Okay, I didn't smell like roses, that was for sure, but I'd smelled far worse than me.

With a shake of my head, I peered around, looking for who he was talking to when little figures began emerging, coming out of the walls themselves. No, not the walls. They dropped out from the shadows, their little dragonfly wings fluttering. My eyes widened as I took them in. Their skin shimmered. It was the same hue of the walls themselves as if they'd camouflaged themselves to blend in with the stone.

Their little bodies, as they drew near, were human

in shape, though they had large black eyes that dominated their face as well as tiny, sharp fangs that peeked out from their mouths as they flew towards me. Any more than the eyes and fangs would have been too much, but it also appeared that they didn't even have noses. The section between their eyes and mouth was not only small but flat and smooth. Each creature was no bigger than the palm of my hand, but they zipped and swooped around me until I began to stumble in the only direction that they had left open to me.

Even as I tried to avoid them, they followed, directing me with their incessant buzzing and fluttering. I turned towards the tunnel I came through when I first found the ballroom, but apparently, they didn't like that because as soon as I took a step in that direction, they swarmed. Small teeth sank into the skin visible on my arms and legs, some latching on as they tried to redirect me, each tooth like sharp tiny needles.

"Ouch!" I cried, glaring at the ones stuck to my skin while trying to remove them without hurting their fragile, little bodies. I pulled and tugged, ripping a few off and letting them go. For every one I pulled off, though, another three latched themselves to my skin until I was more covered in these odd little creatures than not and I had no choice but to admit defeat and let them, quite literally, pull me in the direction they wanted me to go.

They led me through hallways and doors until I was so turned around there wasn't a chance of me ever escaping the castle without help, and I didn't think that the man—God being—whatever, that I had met before was about to give me that help. I'd only just met him, but he struck me as an asshole already. Just my luck, he'd be the first person I ran into in this castle. Oh no, I couldn't run into someone friendly like a little old lady who would pull out a chair and offer me a seat before she piled a plate high with delicious foods for me. Nope. Instead, I got a crusty and mean-faced man —okay, he was handsome, but his personality was seriously lacking.

Finally, the little creatures stopped pulling and released me. Their teeth were even more painful coming out than they had been going in, which just seemed wrong on so many levels. I gasped as each of them withdrew at the same time, my skin stinging sharply from the removal of their little fangs.

When the pain subsided, I was finally able to focus on where I was. With a look, I saw that the room I'd been brought to was as large as a barn, and it was full of giant pools of water. Walls seemed to rise out of the back somewhere and were covered in blues and greens. They were much brighter than the gray stones of the hallway and reminded me of paintings I'd seen of the forest.

The back two pools had steam rising from the surface in billowing clouds and my body ached to sink into that warmth. I hadn't realized how cold I was until that moment. The pool closest to me was my intended location, at least according to the strange little creatures who kept flying from me to the pool and back again.

"Okay, I get it! You want me to get in the water," I muttered more to myself than to actually talk to them, but apparently they didn't see it that way. One of the small creatures came and hovered in front of my face and for the first time, I noticed that it wasn't skin I was seeing as I'd thought before but fine hair all over their bodies. Hair that, if my eyes weren't playing tricks on me, was changing color to blend with this room better. "What are you?" I mused out loud.

"Pixie," one of the creatures growled. The word was barely comprehensible but it was enough. At least, I knew what these little flying demons were now.

"You can talk?" I asked, though the answer was obvious.

The pixie that had spoken just growled and I got the sense that they could understand better than they could speak. We stared at each other for a moment before the creature hissed. It seemed to be a signal for the others because they began swooping down and pulling at my nightdress, tearing the material away from my body with a viciousness that surprised me even after they had been biting me and pulling me to get me into the room.

I had no choice but to stand and let them do whatever it was they were doing. After a few moments they stopped and I felt the remaining few slivers of fabric that had been left slip down my body and pool on the floor.

I was stark naked.

In a strange castle.

What in the name of Coreliath was going on? It was my birthday for the sake of the Gods! Why did it have to be the strangest day of the year? I tried to cover myself with my hands as best as I could but I couldn't seem to cover everything all at once. There was always something left exposed.

The solution, of course, was to get into the water; at least then I'd have some semblance of privacy, even if it wasn't perfect. I dipped my toe into the pool the pixies had been pushing me towards. The icy cold water seemed to suck the remaining heat from my body, leaving my teeth chattering.

There was no freaking way I was getting in that pool.

I padded around the outside, stepping carefully across the rocks that formed the edge of the pools and made my way around to the back. The billows of steam made it almost impossible to see the surface of the water, but I was so cold I didn't care if there was something or someone in there already. I dipped my toe in once again and felt a delicious warmth climb up my skin, one that made me want to climb in and not get out until that warmth had reached the depths of my soul.

Inch by slow inch I descended into the pool, knowing that if I went too fast it would hurt because it was so hot. When it was up to my shoulders I settled back on the underwater bench that seemed to be in place and let myself relax. How could I relax in a strange castle? Well, it wasn't easy. That was for sure. But the heat of the water did steal the tension from my muscles. I moaned and sank down even further. I lifted my arm from the surface of the milky water and let the liquid sluice down my limb. Odd. So very odd. I didn't feel any different than I had the day before. Except that horrible shrieking sound had disappeared. And what a blessing that was.

A moment later, the pixies were putting down bottles on the side of the pool, pushing them towards me. I had no idea what was what so I didn't dare touch them, instead, choosing to eye the little beings with suspicion. The pixies, however, had no such qualms. Two of them picked a bottle, flying over my head—their wings buzzing—and dumped it onto my hair. I gasped reaching up to swat them away, but the damage was done. A third landed on my head and began scrubbing, its pointy, clawed fingers, scraping against my scalp. That ... actually didn't feel that bad. In fact, it was kind of nice.

It continued this way for some time until I felt like a bowl of super warm jelly. When they began to push my head underwater, I knew I was supposed to rinse. What I didn't expect was the sound of voices when I emerged. I froze as two women entered, chatting with one another. Silently praying that they would pass by the bathing room, I held my breath. My luck wasn't that good, it appeared. The door swung open. I could just see the edge of it through the steam so I was able to duck down into the water before anyone could see me.

I was nervous when I had stolen the rolls and the pastry, but now I was terrified. The food had been too much of a treasure to resist. But this was ... I was ... man, I really needed to think my actions through before I did things. Perhaps for the first time in my life, I agreed with the nuns. Had I not followed my instincts here, I would have been ... well, probably about to be kicked out of the convent as soon as everyone realized I was awake.

I shook my head and refocused. I was naked and probably at my most vulnerable with strange women walking towards me. A shriek sounded and I had to fight not to jump out of the water and make a run for it, but the women weren't looking at me, they were too busy sneering in disgust at the pixies.

"Ugh. You know you're not allowed in the baths. Get out! Now, or I'll have your wings torn off!" The woman that screamed had hair the color of starlight and an angular face that looked almost painful with her ivory skin stretched to perfection over the bones of her face. Her naked form strode into one of the pools and I couldn't seem to take my eyes off her. Those were some big ... what had Marcus—the farmer who often frequented the convent called a woman's breasts?—bazoongas?

"What do you think they were doing in here?" the other woman asked, her tone more confused and curious than offended. Peeking up just a little bit more over the edge of the pool I was in, I examined the second woman. Her hair was white at the top, slowly descending into a deep blue at the ends, like frost creeping over the ground. Just like the first woman, she too, was naked. A buzzing noise drew my attention and I turned my head just in time to notice a pixie struggling under the weight of heavy material as it made its way out of the doorway. It wasn't part of my nightdress, so it had to have been whatever clothing these women had shed.

The blue haired woman strode forward into the pool of ice cold water as though it was the perfect temperature. When they were both submerged up to their shoulders they each let out a sigh of what I imagined was relaxation, although they hadn't looked particularly tense when they came in.

"Nasty little creatures were probably using our bathing water," the silver-haired woman said with a shudder. As I watched I realized that it wasn't silver or grey like she was getting old, but more metallic as though she had strands of actual silver spun through her hair.

They were both silent for a moment, soaking in the water, like I had been until they interrupted. I wanted to get out, to move at least, but there was no way to do that without drawing their attention, and something told me I didn't want the type of attention they would give me.

"Did Roan come to you?" the blue-haired woman asked.

"No," the silver-haired woman replied with a frustrated pout before asking, "Did Sorrell come to you?"

"Did he ever. The things that male can do with his cock and his tongue should be illegal," the blue-haired woman said with a dreamy sigh.

I'd never heard anyone talk about sex before and the casualness of their conversation surprised me. I bit my lip. The nuns always made it sound like the moment I saw a cock I'd be condemned to burn for eternity at Coreliath's pleasure. I'd never understood why Coreliath would condemn pleasure like that. It didn't make any sense to me; Gods were known specifically for their own seeking of it. The tales I'd read of the sky God—Zander's—exploits would make anyone blush.

"He wasn't too much this time?" Silver asked, genuine concern filling her voice. I'd decided to think of them as their hair colors since anything else seemed too judgmental on my part.

Blue turned serious for a moment and said, "His cock is massive, of course it's too much, but we work it out. Or more like he works it out on me. He might not be able to fuck me the way he wants, but he sure does make it good. By the Gods, I love screaming his name." Blue giggled and a pang of jealousy ran through me.

Neither of these women looked much older than me and yet they seemed to know so much more about life. I wanted that. I wanted to be worldly and grown-up, not some convent-raised bumpkin that had never even seen a ... what had they called it? A cock? Yeah, I wanted to see that. I smirked to myself. Once I had, maybe I'd go back and tell the nuns all about it. I slid deeper into the water, just picturing the looks of horror on their faces when I did. I wondered if Sister Madeline would even faint.

CHAPTER 7
CRESS

After listening to the two women talk for what felt like hours about their sex lives I was left not only feeling jealous of their romantic relationships but their friendship as well. None of the nuns were my friends, I was too wild for them. The only person who had made an effort over the last few years was Nellie. The other girls, and most of the boys for that matter, at the convent didn't like the negative attention I had received so they'd all given me a wide berth. As if merely being caught by association with me would result in some sort of punishment.

The women continued chatting as they exited the pools and rubbed their bodies with scented oils, which I hadn't even noticed sitting off to the side. They twisted their hair up, creating intricate designs and decorating it with jewels that appeared to be sitting around for anyone to use. Elegance for these two creatures appeared effortless, and my own body felt clunky in comparison. I looked down at my slight frame, palming my breasts. They filled my hands, but not much more. Not compared to theirs. I shot the women a look and sighed.

The kind of friendship these two women had was beyond my understanding. It had always just been me against the world, or the nuns, as it were. I was deep in thought when they left and was startled when a pixie landed on the edge of the pool next to me.

"I don't think you're supposed to be in here," I replied quietly in case the two women were still outside the door.

The pixie simply stuck its little purple tongue out at me and waved at me to follow it. With a grumble, I did as it asked, rising from the warm water and shivering under the coolness of the air. The pixie stopped by the oils and mimed rubbing them on myself. I smiled and nodded to show that I understood and perched on the edge of the bench before opening and smelling each bottle. Floral scents and wood scents, even animal-like scents came from bottle after bottle.

When I saw a dust covered bottle at the back that was almost full I picked it up and gently uncorked it. My nose was greeted by a scent unlike any other I'd tried. It was soft and homey, making me think of being wrapped in safety and light. I began to rub it over my skin, letting the oil sink into my pores and soften my hard edges, if only it would work on my personality as well.

The pixie waved me over to the door when I was

done but I didn't follow, instead, I hissed, "I can't go out there naked!"

It flew away and out of the cracked door before returning with several other pixies that were carrying material. White and gold fabric was hanging between them and I could see various strips and shapes but I had no idea what the piece of clothing was supposed to look like. That didn't matter to the pixies as they swarmed me and pulled the material this way and that, getting way too close to some very personal areas.

By the time they were done, I was in something similar to a dress. The bodice had a wide strip at the front and the back, but the sides were cut out, so my pale flesh was on display from the curve of my breasts to the swell of my hips. Each side had straps attaching to a bra-like piece that cupped my breasts and pushed them up and out in a way that would have made the nun's eyes bug out of their heads. The base of the bra was made of gold fabric and a stripe of it ran over the edges of the V shape in the middle, barely covering my nipples. Straps went up over my shoulders to hold the bra bit in place, but then another set formed something akin to loose sleeves that hung down my upper arms.

The gold returned on my hips outlining the cutout section and forming the trim around the sections of white fabric that hung down in front of me and at the sides. I pulled the fabric and saw that it came apart all the way up to the edge of the cut out, meaning at any point I could be completely exposed since the pixies hadn't bothered to provide underwear. They slid gold slipper like shoes onto my feet, which had a slight rise to them, making me walk on the balls of my feet more than anything else.

Before I knew what they were doing my hair was being styled up and back, so it cascaded down the back of my head like a waterfall. A necklace was looped around my throat and other jewelry was hung from my wrists and ankles. Thick leather straps were wrapped around my thighs, but even those had delicate beads and jewels that hung from them, winking in the light as I moved. It all seemed designed to catch the light, to draw attention to me, which was the last thing I wanted, but since I didn't have any other clothing to wear I was stuck. Maybe I could take the jewelry off later and use it as a distraction while I escaped.

The pixies began to hustle me out of the room through the door, but I paused and they looked at me expectantly as though they didn't want to bite me again but would if I made them. When I remembered the bites I looked down at my arms. There was no trace of any wounds, no signs that anything had happened at all, which just confused me. How had the bites healed so quickly? Maybe it was something in the bathing water? That would explain why Blue was bathing after spending time with some guy with a massive cock.

"Are they out there?" I asked, trying to avoid being bitten but wanting to make sure I wasn't going to be discovered either.

Two of the pixies flew to the door and peeked through the crack between the wood and the stone. They flew back a moment later shaking their heads.

"Okay, fine. Lead the way, but I don't want to get caught. Do you understand?"

The one that seemed to be the leader of their little group nodded.

"Maybe I can sneak you a roll or something later," I said as a thank you.

A wide, fanged smile that looked more vicious than grateful spread over the pixie's face. I decided I'd take that as an agreement and began to follow them back through the winding corridors, hurrying through different rooms and doorways, pausing when they did, just in time to hear the swell of voices coming and going as people seemed to move past me completely unaware of my presence. I couldn't help but wonder if the pixies were literally hiding me. They seemed to have some kind of camouflage ability that they could use, but they wouldn't use that on me, would they? I wasn't sure, and I didn't want to risk our good luck by questioning it if they weren't.

Before I knew it, we were back in the throne room. I could see the man that had commanded the pixies earlier, his dark hair shone with red undertones in the light as he talked with two other men. I froze and gaped. Standing next to the first man were two men of equal stature. Both as tall as the first, but different in color. The second man had a face that had to have been sculpted by the Gods. His features were sharp, angular but in no way unpleasant. He was beauty incarnate. Skin paler than ice with equally pale hair that flowed over his shoulders. Directly in contrast, however, was the third and final man. His face made me want to back up and make a run for it. Hair the color of shadows, strewn with gray and black, with small pale scars littering his olive skin made my heartbeat pick up speed.

Between them—the light and the dark—the man with the red hair appeared to be a shining light, his hair deeper—like freshly spilled wine. He drew my attention just as much as the other two. I couldn't stop flicking my gaze between the three of them as I stood there like a statue. My eyes feasted on the sight of the three of them. Each so different, but so attractive, at least from this distance. Their shirts hung open as though they were comparing who had the best muscles, and their dark pants were tight around their hips and ... my eyebrows rose as I tilted my head. Those butts ... if the Gods knew about these specimens, they'd surely be pissed. The Gods were known for their pride in being the most beautiful of all creatures. But I would be hard pressed to name anything Godly or ungodly that could compare.

Spotting the table of food I'd left behind still piled high, I scurried behind the pillars moving as quickly as I could. As soon as I was close enough, I snatched a couple rolls and tossed them to the pixies before anyone could tell me otherwise. They fell on the food before it even hit the ground in a cloud of fury, all teeth and claws, making me smile as I snatched one for myself and shoved it into my mouth.

"Here's the human. See? Not dead after all," the red-haired man from before spoke. I turned my head slowly—cheeks ballooned by the food in my mouth. He sounded much more jovial than before. I narrowed my eyes on him in suspicion as I chewed and swallowed.

The red haired man strode down the steps of what looked to be a platform at the back of the room complete with not one, not two, but three lavish thrones. He moved with a grace I'd never possessed in my life. Though he was a veritable giant, he moved across the room with a speed and agility that spoke of confidence. At his back, the others followed.

Perhaps a smarter person would have realized the danger I was in and would have been ready to run. I had, after all, broken into a strange castle that had shown up out of nowhere. I had left my entire life behind with little regard for where it would leave me. I should have been scared; however, in direct contrast with what I knew I should've been feeling, my mouth watered.

"You said she was hideous," the white-haired man muttered. "And that she stank of the human realm." Eyes the color of crystallized frost raked over my form. "I don't detect that odor, though." I stared at him just as much as he stared at me, curiosity warring with intrigue.

"She did," the red-haired man agreed. "I had her

cleaned." His nose wrinkled as he examined me from head to toe. "She was absolutely filthy before. This is a considerable improvement." The red-haired man's eyes slid to the side where I'd tossed a few of the rolls to the pixies. I followed his gaze. There was nothing left now, but I wondered if he'd caught me. I stiffened as he moved closer, leaning down into my personal space. When he smiled, it was decidedly threatening, but instead of speaking to me, he threw a question over his shoulder. "What do you think, Orion?"

The shadowed man answered. "I still smell human on her skin," he said, his tone a low growl, like boulders crashing together. "But there's something else. It's not unpleasant." Eyes the color of burned stone met mine. "In fact, I'd say she smells good enough to eat."

"Eat?" I squeaked. Were they going to eat me? I glanced nervously between the three of them. "I-I thought you wanted answers from me," I said quickly, hoping they'd vie against wanting to eat me in favor of getting the red-haired man's questions answered.

"True." The red-haired man lifted a strand of my pale hair and sniffed at it delicately. "It should have been impossible for a human to not only find our castle, but to enter it without any warning." His fingers slid the rest of the way into my hair, locking onto my scalp and drawing it back as a fire burned brighter in his eyes. He stared down at me, his smile twisting into something cruel.

My body reacted to the tone of his voice, but not in the way I'd expected. Instead of struggling to get away,

I leaned forward. What would it feel like to have those teeth against my skin? Those lips moving over my own?

Orion, the dark man, stepped up alongside his red friend. "She must be some human," he said, tilting his head to the side as he gazed down at me. Never before had I held such attention. It was both terrifying and thrilling. My body practically vibrated with it, as if screaming *oh my Gods, someone's looking at me! What do I do?*

The red-haired man's smile widened and Nellie's warning chose that moment to come barreling through my mind full throttle. *They're otherworldly,* she'd said. *Beautiful and savage.* Just like these men who were, perhaps, not men at all.

I stared at the man before me, directly at his full lips. They were a deep ruby color and looked softer than anything I'd ever felt before. My desire to find out brought me even closer to him. I lifted on my tiptoes as I reached up. I wanted to feel, to find out if they were as soft as I thought they were. He frowned down at me, those very lips curling down as he watched my movements. The fire that had been ignited in the depth of his eyes burned ever brighter, drawing me like a moth to a flame. No good could come from messing with it, and yet I was willing to burn my wings anyway just to find out.

CHAPTER 8
CRESS

"*Stop*." I jerked back just before my fingers brushed his lips. The man before me turned his cheek, towards the one who'd spoken. White hair flashed at my side, cold fingers gripping my arm as the third man—the one with hair as white as snow—pulled me away. "She's human or did you forget, Roan?"

Roan? I looked back at the red-haired man. His name was Roan? The same Roan the two women had been talking about. I looked to the shadowed man. If black was Orion, red was Roan, then ... my unspoken thoughts were answered a moment later as Roan replied.

"I haven't forgotten, Sorrell," he growled.

"Then what do you think you're doing?" His fingers tightened against my upper arm, squeezing roughly. I winced. *Damn that hurt*. I waited a moment, letting the two of them do their whole eye-stare-glare nonsense before I got tired of it.

"Um, excuse me?" I politely tapped the man holding me—Sorrell. He glanced down, white eyebrows shooting up as if he was just now realizing that I could speak. That's right, buddy, I talk. "You're hurting me," I told him. "Do you think you could..." I lifted my arm, the very one that he still held, and looked at it pointedly.

He released me almost immediately. So abruptly that I stumbled and nearly fell over. I shook my head and sent him a dirty look. *Was that really necessary?* But he didn't even notice. Sorrell whirled on his friend, a frown marring his otherwise perfect features. "What are you going to do about this disaster?" he demanded, gesturing back at me. I looked down. I'd taken a bath. I looked a lot nicer than I had before. I wasn't a disaster, at least, not by appearances anymore. How rude.

"He does have a small point," the dark one—Orion—said. "What if others found out that our Court was breached? There would be a riot."

"No one will find out," Roan said. "We'll question her and have her executed with no one the wiser."

"Executed!" I squeaked. "Don't I get a say?" Three very different colored gazes settled on me.

"A say?" the dark one repeated.

"Yeah," I said. "I don't think I've done anything to warrant death. So, I should get a say."

"You broke into our Court," Roan said with a scowl. "That is a treasonous offense."

"But I didn't know I was breaking in," I defended. "The doorway just opened on its own! When I went to turn back, it was gone." I huffed and puffed, my face heating as the three of them exchanged a look before fixating back on me. The weight of their stares made my whole body tense. I didn't know what to expect from them next.

"That ... you're sure that's what happened?" the white one asked. Man, I really needed to get a bead on them. White. Black. Red. Sorrell. Orion. Roan. I knew their names, but for some reason, I kept fixating on their colors. Maybe I'd just call them by their color. That would make things easier. At least, it would for me.

I nodded. "Of course, why would I lie?"

Orion came towards me, curling his lip back intimidatingly. "There are many reasons why one would lie. To harm. To deceive. To escape their fate."

I gulped before I crossed my arms over my chest in what was hopefully a tough gesture. "Well, I'm not," I stated, hoping my voice sounded strong and defiant and not breathy.

He flipped his head towards Roan. "You're sure she's human?"

"Smell her yourself, she smells completely human to me," he said sliding a hand my way.

"Whoa!" I put my hands out. "You already sniffed my hair. No one else is *smelling* me! That's weird. You can't just smell someone; it's rude." I looked pointedly at Roan.

"It's either that or you die," Sorrell said carefully, arching a brow my way.

I shoved my arm out. On second thought ... "Well, if you're going to be that way..." I said. "Sniff away. While you're doing that, my name is Cress, by the way. I feel like you should know my name if you're going to be sniffing me and all that."

The dark Fae didn't say anything as his fingers gripped my wrist, his massive hands engulfing my much smaller limb as he dipped his head. His eyes remained on mine. I sucked in a breath as he pressed the tip of his nose to the inner crook of my arm and ran it slowly upward as he inhaled. Tingles raced through my flesh where we were connected—and startlingly, the space between my legs tightened and grew wet. I clenched my thighs. *Dangerous*, I thought. *These men were very, very dangerous.*

Orion hummed in his throat. "Her scent is weak," he said, the words vibrating against my flesh. "The human smell is there, but there's something beneath it." He lifted his head and stared at me. "What region are your parents from?" he demanded.

"I—um ... don't..." I swallowed roughly before continuing. "I'm an orphan," I admitted. "I don't know who my parents are or where they're from."

"What if she's a Changeling?" Sorrell said suddenly, looking to Roan.

Roan shook his head, red locks sliding over his temple as he moved. "There hasn't been a Changeling in years," he said. "The last Court that participated in that ridiculous ritual was..." He stopped, frowning as he lifted his head and stared straight at me. With so much attention on me—far more than I was used to—I was starting to develop a complex. I kept feeling like there was something on my face.

"What?" I asked as Orion's fingers released me enough so that I could take a step back from all three of them. My flight reflex was screaming inside of me. But along with it, there was another instinct telling me to move closer to these three. There was something magnetic about them.

"How old are you?" Roan asked, striding through the others until he reached me, hovering dangerously close, smelling like fire and cinder.

My head tilted back. "I'm ... uh ... my birthday is today. I-I'm twenty-one." The words stuttered out as my eyebrows inched slowly upward.

"It's impossible," Sorrell said. "The Brightling Court was exterminated. All of them. There were no survivors."

"Orion has the best nose out of all of us; if he agrees with your Changeling idea then she could be," Roan replied.

Orion nodded slowly, seeming to turn the idea over in his mind.

"What's a Changeling?" I asked before I let myself get too distracted by Orion's dark intelligence.

Instead of answering, however, the three turned

towards each other and began to speak in low tones. I gaped at them for a moment as they talked fast and quiet. Every once in a while, one of them would lift their head and look at me before returning to the others.

"Then it's decided," Roan said, standing up fully once more as they all pivoted back to me.

"What's decided?" I asked. I really hoped they weren't going to kill me. Or eat me. Neither of those things would work for my future plans—which all depended on me remaining alive. "I haven't decided anything," I said quickly. "So, nothing's been decided. Do you hear me? Nothing!"

"You'll join our Court," he said. "We'll have to completely eradicate your scent, imprint one of ours on you, and then we'll put you through a series of tests to determine if you are, in fact, a Changeling."

"And how exactly are you going to do that?" I asked. "Eradicate my scent that is?"

Roan stepped forward and gripped my wrist when I would have stumbled away. "The fastest way would be for me to lay with you. Come, we'll take care of that right now."

"Wait, what!" I shrieked as he dragged me towards the exit. I grabbed onto his arm and tried to pry my wrist from his grip even as I kicked at his legs. "You can't just—urg! Why don't you—for the love of the Gods, *what* are you made of?" He was pure freaking mountain beneath my struggles, pausing only when he realized I wasn't falling all over myself and jumping to get him in bed. "Listen, buddy," I snapped, "we can't have sex. I mean, don't get me wrong, I want to have sex. I'd like to know what it's like because the nuns said it was a sin and I've come to learn that anything the nuns deem as sinful is actually pretty fun. They said it was sinful to eat too much, but eating is awesome, especially if the food tastes good..." Three sets of eyes stared at me unblinkingly. "Anyway..." I waved my hand in front of my face, "you're right, that's not the point. The point *is*—you can't just decide something like that on your own."

"Would you prefer Orion or Sorrell?" he asked.

"What?" I looked over my shoulder at them. "Maybe..." I said, eyeing Sorrell's form and then Orion's before shaking my head. "I mean no!" *What was I doing?* "That's not—I wasn't trying to choose someone else."

"Then you will lay with me," he stated as if it was a given conclusion.

I eyed him. "You're really full of yourself, aren't you?"

He shrugged, but his hand never released me. "I am quite accomplished in the task of bedding and pleasuring women. You will enjoy yourself."

"I'm a virgin!" No sooner had I shrieked that very embarrassing truth than a woman came through the entrance of the throne room—one of the women from earlier, the one with the silver hair and perfect face. She stopped dead, her mouth dropping as she took in the scene before her.

"M-my Lord?" she stammered.

I groaned and slapped my face. This day really wasn't working out. I needed to find a bed, crawl in it, and hope that when I woke up, this whole thing would blow over and be nothing but a terrible dream.

CHAPTER 9
ROAN

Of course. Of. Fucking. Course. Ariana had to walk in right then, didn't she? Because why would the Goddess ever do anything to assist me?

"Lady Ariana, how are you this morning?" Sorrell asked, dipping his head in greeting.

"Is that a human?" she demanded pointing at the woman in my arms.

"If you want to live, don't leave this spot and don't say a word," I whispered as I set the female down, though I could feel her quaking in my arms. For a moment, I thought the human might fall over, so I kept a hand on her waist to keep that from happening. The action did not go unnoticed as it drew a glare from Ariana as her eyes focused directly on where my palm rested on the human's side. I could tell from the way she had dressed—as if she were about to attend one of my mother's signature balls rather than simply walk through the Court—that she was upset I hadn't come to her after we had moved the castle. Expending so much stamina required a boost of magic and Fae were known for their voracious sexual appetites, specifically to lift our magical energy.

"Darling Ariana, I didn't expect you to be up this early," I crooned at her as I released the other female.

"Clearly." She crossed her arms over her more than ample chest, and I wondered what had kept me from burying my cock in her when I'd had the chance. At the very least, it would have avoided this whole mess with the ... Changeling. I let my eyes slide down over her luscious curves, noting the way her gaze slid to the front of my trousers and the growing bulge there. She was a scrumptious little piece ... when she kept her mouth shut that is. Ariana smirked just enough to let me know I was off the hook for not coming to her chambers. "Is that a human?" she asked again, but this time she sounded far more scandalized than furious as she leaned around trying to get a peek at the creature. I shoved the girl behind me.

"Changeling. We suspected a few in the area, which is why we stopped the castle here," I lied through my teeth, gritting them in a facsimile of an actual smile. "An investigation needs to be made before we continue on." No reason to tell her that we had all but spent our magical reserves, and if we hadn't stopped here then the castle certainly would have crash landed somewhere completely off the grid of our maps. And I saw no reason to tell her how the possible Changeling had infiltrated our castle either. Ariana was born of the High Court for sure, but she was no princess.

"But ... that's practically unheard of!" Her eyes had gone wide and she stepped closer, craning her elegant neck even more.

I lowered my voice conspiratorially as I took a step forward—towards Ariana and away from the Changeling. "We aren't sure how much a threat they are so I wouldn't get too close. Don't want you getting hurt by some filth." I hooked my hand around her waist before she could pass me and brought my lips to her cheek in a delicate kiss, while my hand slid down the front of her dress to cup her through the front of her gown. "You're much too precious to risk. Now, why don't you wait for me in your chambers and as soon as I get this creature secured, I'll come and pay tribute." I nipped her ear and moved down her neck, my lips and teeth working her skin between words as I spoke, while my fingers danced against the space between her legs through the fabric of her dress.

Her silver eyes caught mine as I began to pull away. "Don't let me down, Roan, I need you to finish what you started here," she said, her voice husky with need. She licked her lips.

"As my lady commands." I brushed my lips against hers before I turned and headed back towards the Changeling. The clicking of Ariana's heeled shoes sounded in my ear as she left the room.

I was surprised to find the girl's face paler than it had been when I first saw her and anger dancing in her gaze. Before I spoke, I glanced over my shoulder just to be sure the other woman had gone. Now that she was taken care of, I could return to the matter at hand, at least momentarily, until I needed to go and bed the needy Faerie.

"Masterfully done," Sorrell complimented with a cool raised brow. Orion hummed his agreement.

I nodded my thanks. My ability to bend Ariana to my will was probably one of my most treasured talents. She could be a thorn in the side if I wasn't careful, but as long as I kept her compliant she was more like a flower. Pretty and amenable when all of her thorns had been trimmed.

My gaze traveled over the Changeling once more, and I took in every detail. She was quite different from Ariana in many ways. Where Ariana was buxom and curvaceous, this girl was lithely muscular, with a tautness to her skin that spoke of youth and physical activity that was certainly closer to work than anything Ariana would ever do in her lifetime. I knew from experience, Ariana's nipples were quite round, a dark rose. Staring down at the possible Changeling woman, noting the way her nipples poked at the fabric of her dress, I wondered what color hers would be. Perhaps a light pink. A cherry red? She might prove to be quite interesting if she was, in fact, a Changeling. If she was human, then she would be executed without question. As was custom.

"Come, let's get the remaining human scent off you," I said as I went to scoop her back up.

"You—you can't seriously expect me to give you my virginity when we just met!" she said suddenly. "And you were just seducing another woman. I'm not stupid, even if you did fuck me—you'd surely go right to her. How do I know you don't have some kind of disease?"

I looked at her, clearly the idea of being bedmates offended her, but to accuse me of disease ... I growled low in my throat. "Fae do not contract human disease," I snapped. Humans were strange creatures. Maybe she had been taught humankind's tight-laced sense of propriety. I sighed, done playing games with the Changeling until she could answer some basic questions. "If you refuse me, then pick either Orion or Sorrell and be done with it. Virginity is not the end all, be all in the Fae Courts; in fact, you are more likely to be looked down on for being so prudish. The society you were born to be a part of—"

"If she is actually a Changeling," Sorrell reminded me.

"The society you may have been born to be a part of is one that runs on pleasure," I continued without comment. "Pleasure of food, drink, flesh, you name it, we know how to find pleasure in it. The only thing we don't find pleasure in is humans. Now, make your choice." I gestured to the two men standing off to my right.

She just gaped at me and I had to wonder if her time spent with the humans had impacted her development, because she seemed awfully slow to pick up on ideas or take action.

"Orion," she said eventually.

I had expected fear or trepidation in her voice, but none came. It was calm and steady, just like her form. Her Changeling nature was already asserting itself, I knew it. The fact that I was right, not that my friends would admit it yet, was like a balm to my frazzled nerves. Now I just had to go and make Ariana forget that she had ever seen the Changeling and everything would be fine. With a nod to my friend, I turned and walked away.

CHAPTER 10
CRESS

What trouble had I found myself in this time? The nuns were always telling me I was dangerous, that I'd put the others in jeopardy with my actions, but I'd never expected anything like this to happen the first time I ventured away from the convent. The two remaining Fae were staring down at me like I was a bug trapped under a glass. I had opted for Orion since I hadn't heard any horror stories about him yet or watched him practically shove his hand up another woman's skirts right in front of me. But even as I looked over at him—I was doubting my choice. Of all three of them, he was the scariest. Shadows seemed to cling to his very skin, highlighting the darkness in his gaze as well as the numerous scars that peeked out from beneath his shirtsleeves and collar. I knew better than to think any of them were safe.

Besides, if I was what they claimed—a Changeling—then would I be allowed to leave when we were done? If I did, where would I go? It wasn't like the nuns were going to welcome me back with open arms, not unless I gave my vows and joined them, which was never going to happen. *I mean, seriously, a life of chastity? For someone like me? Not happening.*

"Shall we?" Orion said as he offered me his arm like he was a knight in shining armor and I was a princess from a fairytale. I blinked dumbly at it before reaching forward, hesitantly and letting my hand wrap around his bicep. *Oh Gods, he had some muscles.* I squeezed lightly, admiring the thickness of his arm. Orion smirked down at me and I paused, having been caught. I pursed my lips and turned my head away as heat warmed my cheeks.

With little other to look at, my gaze landed on Sorrell. The heat from Sorrell's stare as he looked at our joined arms speared me. The expression accompanying that heat was ... enigmatic. I couldn't tell if he was happy, angry, sad, or ... I couldn't tell anything from the way he was looking at us. His face was just a blank mask, reminding me of the perfect sheet of ice that used to form on the water bucket for the pigs at the convent. His pale blue eyes met mine briefly before he turned and stormed away, his steps echoing loudly up the throne room walls. I guess that meant he was angry. *Had I insulted him by choosing Orion? How was I supposed to know?*

Orion had started walking though, and if I didn't want to fall flat on my face, I needed to move or he might just drag me along behind him. I had been hauled plenty of places in my life by the nuns, and sliding along the ground with your face in the dirt wasn't a good look for anyone. I started walking, taking a couple longer strides to catch up until we fell into an easy rhythm that wasn't too slow for him or too fast for me. Why was I focusing on walking so much? Oh, yeah, because this guy was supposed to take my virginity, something which the nuns had drilled into me was sacred. *I wondered how one took someone's virginity and why was it called taking and giving? Was it such a big deal?* Roan hadn't seemed to think it was.

It had never made sense to me—the invisible status of someone's *innocence* that supposedly made the nuns better than everyone else, more devoted to their faith, when yet their other behaviors were often so different. While some of the nuns had been kind, there were those like Sister Madeline who were harsh and often cruel, violent, and quick to punish. But the fact that they had saved themselves from temptations of the flesh somehow absolved all of that? That was a big steaming pile of horse manure if I ever heard one. And if that was the case—if having this unsatisfied need inside you made the nuns twisted and mean— then I would gladly give up my virginity and keep my sanity.

"What are you thinking about?" The question came from the man holding me and when I looked up into his obsidian eyes, I panicked.

"Horse manure," I blurted.

He nearly tripped over his own two feet and took

me down with him. Barely managing to catch himself in time, he slid his arm away from mine and caught me by the waist to keep from tumbling to the floor. I blinked. So did he. His lids slowly lowered and then lifted. I focused on his lashes—why the hell were they so long and beautiful? In fact, all of him was beautiful—even with the lines of white scars marring his skin. He just had this otherworldliness to him—probably a Fae aspect.

"I am about to bed you and you're thinking of ... horse shit?"

"Well, to be fair, I wasn't thinking about the fact that you're going to have—I mean you're gonna do ... you know, *that*," I emphasized without using the actual term. "I mean, I was, but I wasn't thinking that you were going to be horse shit at it, I was just—"

He placed a palm over my mouth, his brows lowered together—nearly touching as he frowned. "Do you ever stop talking?"

"Yes," I replied, the sound muffled behind his massive paw. I turned my cheek and slid my face out from beneath his hand. "I have to sleep sometime, don't I?"

He just continued to stare at me. I wondered if he didn't realize that humans actually had to sleep. "You do know that humans sleep, right?" I asked. "I mean, if I am human that is. Fae sleep too, right? Or do you guys just like..." I trailed off, reaching up with both hands and placed my fingers above my eyes, stretching the skin slightly so it'd look like I was peeling my eyeballs open.

The frown didn't leave his face. "You are a strange creature," he finally said with a shake of his head. We continued down the hallway, but his hand never left my hip—anchoring me to the side of his body beneath his arm. Gods, he was like a fire—burning hot. I was already sweating. I could feel little sweat beads popping up along my temple and my upper lip. They slid down the small of my back even through the little skimpy dress as it fluttered around me leaving me feeling like I didn't have enough air.

Our feet tapped against the flagstone tiles of the floor while I tried to wrap my head around the events that had just transpired—both the stuff that had already happened and what was about to happen. I wondered what time it was. We hadn't passed a single window since we'd set off from the throne room. The walls that surrounded us now were dark, almost as dark as Orion's hair, which I swear looked more like it was absorbing light than reflecting it like mine usually did. Cool blonde strands fluttered in front of my face and I blew them out of the way. Flames flickered on torches that were dotted along the hallway, but the light never seemed to reach far beyond the torch itself.

Occasionally, I caught a glimpse of a door, the thick wood looking bright in comparison to the dark, deep gray of everything else. Sometimes the light was reflected enough that I was fairly sure the walls were made of a dark marble or something similar. They weren't regular brick or stone, of that much I was sure. As we moved through the dark halls in silence, my mind began to focus on my other senses and I caught a whiff of something dark and exotic. Bergamot and jasmine mixed with something woodsy that made me think of the forest that was just at the edge of the convent grounds.

I took a deep breath, soaking in the delicious fragrance. If I could bottle the way he smelled, I'd make a fortune in a fortnight.

"Did you just smell me?" Orion asked, his voice a low rumble that was barely audible even though I was standing right next to him.

Heat flared back to life in my face. "You did it to me first," I said defensively. It hadn't been intentional, but damn I couldn't help doing it again, inhaling the scent wafting from his skin.

Once again, he shook his head. "Here." He stopped before an alcove, reaching forward and finding the door's handle beyond in the shadows. His hand turned and the door opened, creaking softly as it swung inward. I gulped, wanting to back away, but he was already ushering me inside, the door closing behind us and sealing us into a room full of shadows and darkness.

The room we entered was even darker than the hallway. So pitch black that I put my hands out, afraid that I would run into a wall or something. There was a shifting sound at my back and then I felt Orion move around me, and as he did, lights began to flicker to life, illuminating the room. Flames danced behind glass vases anchored to the walls, casting around as if each light spurred the next one on until the whole room was bathed in the warm glow.

Even though I saw the lights flare and come to life, I had no idea how they were doing so. There was no switch, no flame in Orion's hand. It was ... pure magic. Fae magic, I realized. "Holy horse shit," I whispered. Orion paused, his back to me before casting a look back. "What?" I asked.

He didn't say anything, though, and I returned to gazing at the wonder of the flames.

They reflected off the walls, but instead of the charcoal gray I'd expected, a deep indigo color with a hint of violet was reflected back. Gold filigree decorated the edges and corners of the walls, drawing my eyes up to the most impressive ceiling I'd ever seen. Something twinkled, embedded in the rafters above me. The longer I stared at it the more I realized it was constellations. Somehow the stars seemed to shine through the castle and into Orion's bedroom. My eyes caught on a large, yet delicate, painting of the moon on the ceiling and I became even more fascinated.

"How..." I whispered, but didn't know what to ask so my voice trailed off into nothingness.

"Glass, embedded in the ceiling, but if you come over here you can see the real thing," Orion said from the base of a spiral staircase I hadn't even noticed yet. My feet carried me towards him without me even thinking about it. On the way, I passed a massive bed, one that could easily sleep all of the children at the convent with room to spare. A large cornice stuck out in the shape of a crown, hanging over half the bed with long velvety curtains slipping from the top to the edge of the bed.

Next to the bed was a small library of books and cushioned chairs. A large structure sat in the center of the space. It was made up of multiple rings, all attached to one another in the shape of a globe, with a small sphere at the center. It was fascinating to look at, especially as the gold of the structure glinted in the light showing that there were markings and words on it that I was too far away to read.

A soft clearing of a masculine throat drew my attention away from the many books and the structure I had started towards without even realizing it. I froze mid-step and pouted as I considered whether or not to ignore the Fae at my back and continue towards my objective or answer the obvious call he'd administered. It took several heartbeats for me to come to a decision, and with a sigh, I put my foot down and turned back to Orion. He arched one brow before gesturing to the staircase. My eyes rounded. Abandoning all caution, I made a straight line for the bottom of it and began to climb. I marveled as it twisted around over itself until it came out to the most breathtaking sight.

My jaw dropped as that familiar scent that I'd caught on Orion's body met me. Flowers. Dozens of them lined up in rows. He had a garden above his bedroom. It was surrounded by glass walls and topped with a domed glass ceiling that had the most intricate lead work I had ever seen. Nothing like anything the convent possessed. The room made it look like it was still nightfall, but was it? Hadn't the sun been coming up as I'd come into the castle? Looking beyond the lead that made captivating patterns in the glass I was able to see the stars for real this time.

"Beautiful, is it not?" Orion asked, leading me along a path that ran between tall plants, the likes of which I had never seen before.

"I ... don't know what to say. It's stunning," I breathed, still staring up at the dome while simultaneously trying not to miss any of the gorgeous flowers we were passing and stay on the path so I didn't crush any of his plants.

"Here, have a seat," he said as he gestured to where a large blanket and pillows were laid out on the ground. The patch had evidently been kept clear for a time and I got the feeling that this was a more personal space than he might admit. I slid a glance his way. If it was, why would he be showing me this when we'd only just met? Before I could think about it too hard, though, I moved to where he'd waved me. I didn't just sit; I laid back on the blanket and stared up, watching the stars and trying to orient myself. A difficult task to be sure, but one that was all encompassing. I couldn't tear my eyes away.

"It's a different sky than the one you're used to seeing," he said quietly.

I glanced up and caught him watching me, a small smile tugging at his lips. "It is?" I asked.

"This room channels night. No matter where we are or what time it is, the windows only show night whether it's from where the castle is at that moment or somewhere it has been that is currently experiencing night." He paused for a second as I just stared at him with my mouth agape. "All the flowers and plants in this room flourish during the night time, so you can experience them whenever you want."

I started to speak, a million questions fluttered in my head all at once, but none of them came out. Instead, I squeaked. A friggin' squeak. Like a mouse. I covered my face with my hands and moaned in awkward embarrassment.

"You said you're a virgin, and I want to respect that, but if you wish to survive this place, then we can't risk anyone mistaking you for a human," he said as he sat on the blanket next to me, his long limbs stretching out next to mine as he leaned close to me. Orion was massive, far bigger than the few men I'd seen regularly in my life. Larger than the butcher that delivered food to the convent. Larger than the blacksmith that I'd seen in the local village. Each of his features—from his hands to his whole body radiated heat and strength. He was big enough to break me, I knew, and it should have scared me. In a way, it did. But not to the extent I expected, that it was supposed to. His dark eyes seemed to glow in the moonlight and from this proximity I could see flecks of gray and white, as though I was looking into the night sky itself in his eyes. The effect was only enhanced by the long strands of hair that hung down over his shoulder, creating an ebony backdrop for his sparkling eyes.

The weight of reality crashed down around me once more when his words finally registered. My eyes snapped away from his but caught on his open shirt. Stretched out next to me like this I could see all the tiny scars that covered his body along with the depth of color in his skin. It wasn't just olive as I had thought earlier; there was a different kind of darkness there as well, whether it was the color of smoke or slightly more purple, it seemed to swirl over his skin like the ocean, constantly changing course and shifting. I couldn't help but notice his muscular frame as well, lean and strong, I wanted to bite my lip as I took it in, especially as my eyes lingered over the way his pants fit around his ass and thighs. *Was this what lust felt like?*

His dark eyes watched me as I checked him out; I could feel them on me as surely as a caress, and it made my body hum with need. My mind threw the memory of his smelling me earlier back at me, the soft feeling of his skin against my own and I wondered what it would feel like to kiss his full lips, to feel his touch on other parts of my body. Just the thought of it set my heart galloping in my chest as we stared at each other.

CHAPTER 11
ORION

Females were such intriguing creatures and this one was no different. Though, perhaps, she was a bit more interesting than most. Her small pert little nose tilted up as she stared at the ceiling of my secret garden. Her eyes glittered, reflecting the millions of fragments of pseudo-moonlight—a spell of my own making.

She was so small, soft—fragile. Her scent as a human was weak after Roan had ordered her cleaned but still there. Likely, it had seeped into her skin after all the years she'd spent in their realm. I leaned closer to her and when she didn't pull away, I knew she would accept this. I pressed small, chaste kisses to her temple. Something, I'd never done for any female. This one wasn't just any female though. She was special. She'd chosen me—over Sorrell, over Roan. Something the other women of the Court hadn't done.

My fingers trailed down her arm, circling her wrist

and bringing it up so that she wound the limb around my neck as I moved my face lower. "It may hurt at first," I whispered into the quiet of the room. "But after the initial pain, I will ensure you feel only pleasure."

"Does it have to hurt?" she asked. "I mean, can't you just like ... make me think it doesn't? You're a Fae. Fae have magical powers."

I smirked as I pressed another one of those close-mouthed kisses to the underside of her jaw. Her heart picked up pace as it beat a consistent rhythm. I could feel it pounding, hear it in my ears as well as I could scent the telltale sign of her arousal. Her legs shifted and when I pulled her onto my lap, wrapping those legs around my waist, that scent blossomed and became heavier—overwhelming the scent of the flowers surrounding us.

"Different types of Fae have different types of powers, and that is not one I possess," I confessed as I parted my lips and licked a path up her throat. Her spine bowed as if she wanted to arch away, but as soon as I pulled away, she pressed closer—her breasts crushed against my chest. I chuckled, and the sound reverberated through both of our bodies. "If I could take your pain away, little one, I would."

Her breath hitched as I cupped her backside, pulled her so that the center of her was pressed to my groin. I knew she would feel how hard I already was—it'd been quite a while since I'd bedded a female like this. Amber eyes flickered at me, her lashes throwing shadows across her cheeks. Shadows I called to me, stealing from her and leaving her in nothing but illuminating moonlight. Her skin glowed, iridescent and beautiful. Cool and smooth like ivory, soft like nothing I'd ever known. I would enjoy taking this creature to my bed, I knew. I would ensure she enjoyed it too.

I turned, placing her back against the cushions and blankets as I came down on top of her. We were like light and dark, and I wondered briefly if that faint hint of otherness I'd caught a whiff of—the very thing that made me stop Roan from immediately demanding her execution—really was of the Brightling Court. A Court that had perished in the war nearly the same time as she would've been born. She had no clue—that much was obvious. But then the Brightling Court had been far more tolerant of humans than any other Court—to their demise.

I shook my head and pressed a kiss to her lips, parting my mine and letting my tongue dip between hers. She tasted of a freshness that was uniquely her. I rolled my hips as I dug my fingers into her sides. She was such a slight little thing. If I wasn't careful I'd snap her in half. She, on the other hand, didn't seem at all worried about it.

A low moan rumbled out of her throat as she pressed her hips up into mine and when her eyes crossed my face, they were clouded with surprise and lust. I had to remind myself that she was untouched, she would not appreciate being thrust into like a fast adolescent. It would not just hurt, but likely make her unwilling to do it again and I wanted to sample this beauty many more times after tonight if she was, in fact, a Changeling.

The female was a quick study. In no time at all, she was arching her hips into mine, rubbing herself wantonly—moaning as she, too, thrust her tongue into my mouth. She was mimicking me, I realized. Taking everything I gave her and giving it back. Tenfold. I pulled back and gritted my teeth as she nearly came off the floor as she pressed into me. My cock was stiff beneath my trousers and I knew I needed to slow things down if I was to make this as good for the little virgin as I wanted to.

Reaching back, I removed her legs from around my waist and set her feet down flat on the floor. Her eyes, which had been lowered halfway, popped open. She blinked at me, frowning in confusion. "What is it?" she asked. "Did I mess up? Did I do something wrong?"

I shook my head, lifting my tunic up and over my head. I tossed the fabric to the side, moving back to her as my hands went to the strips of fabric covering her small breasts. I froze at the look of utter astonishment on her face. I looked down. *Was it the scars?* I wondered. She'd seen them through the opening, surely she wouldn't be shocked.

But no, she wasn't shocked. She was curious, I realized a moment later as she sat up, her hands moving to my skin. Her fingers ran through the matt of hair that covered my chest. She followed it down to the line that trailed into the waistband of my pants. I inhaled sharply, capturing her wandering hand in one of mine before she could go too far. Dangerous. This little Changeling was dangerous.

I took the hand she'd been exploring with and placed it down on the pillows, holding it there with one of my own as I reached for her other arm. I couldn't take any chances with this girl. Capturing and keeping both of her hands above her head, I used my free hand to untie the strips of fabric covering her breasts. Slipping one away and pulling it free from her body, I used it to tie her hands together.

"Keep those there for me," I commanded. Big, wondrous eyes stared at me. "Do you understand, little one?" I asked when she didn't reply. "Keep your hands above your head and I'll give you a gift," I said, pinching her chin between my thumb and forefinger as I stared down into her gaze.

"What will you give me?" she countered.

I laughed. "The stars," I said. A promise.

She looked up at the ceiling. "You kind of already did that."

Another laugh. "Different stars," I assured her. "Ones you can't see any other way."

She stared at me, narrowing her gaze slightly as if in suspicion. I waited, nonetheless, for the small but perceptive nod of acquiescence. Once I had that, I left her chin, pressing a kiss to the center of her chest. She inhaled as if just realizing that her breasts were bared to my gaze. Her nipples peaked beneath my palms as I skated both of my hands over the small but plump mounds. I squeezed each before circling with my fingers, first pinching one pretty pink bud before doing the same to the other. Her breath came in ragged pants. Her stomach sucked in and out. Her legs shifted beneath me.

I moved further down, removing the rest of her dress as I went until she was wholly and completely naked before me. "W-what are you doing?" She gasped as I pressed an open mouthed kiss to the inside of one thigh, lifting it until I could see the spot between her legs that called to me. Oh it was pretty. A nice pink just like her nipples.

"Taking you to paradise, little one," I whispered back just as I leaned forward and gave her my mouth. I sucked the needy little bud that poked out between her lower lips and relished in her cry of pleasure. She arched up, her hands coming down immediately—fingers spearing into the hair at the back of my head. That was alright. I'd been doubtful of her ability to hold back with my mouth on her. I liked it, in fact. Loved the feeling of a woman losing control beneath me.

I licked and sucked at her like I was eating the juiciest of fruits. My tongue swiped a path up the center of her before delving deeper. She shivered, panted, and moaned. Wetness oozed down my chin as I licked some more, fighting to catch as much of the delicious juice as I could. When her thighs tightened around my head, I reached up and shoved her wide open—eliciting a cry of surprise.

She shivered beneath me, the whole of her body

fighting upward every time I pulled away to catch a breath. It was as if she couldn't stand for me to be away. I grinned, sliding up so that my shoulders blocked her from tightening her thighs once more. With my fingers, I spread her pretty lower lips and then gently touched the small opening that would soon take my cock. She was so small there. Tiny. Vulnerable.

I licked her essence from my lips as I slipped first one finger inside and then a second. She clamped down around the digits, squirming as her eyes looked up at me in awe. I loved that look on a woman's face just before I showed her the other side of paradise.

Holding her gaze, I let my head descend once more. I pumped my fingers in and out as I licked that needy bud once more. A moment—two—passed. I couldn't tell if she was even breathing. She could feel it, though. That much I did know. She could sense what was about to happen.

Slowly. Ever so slowly, I pulled my fingers clear from her passage, added a third and held them positioned just inside the opening. I didn't wait or give her any warning. I sucked her bud into my mouth at the same time that I shoved them forward, curling them towards me in a fast, hard motion. And the expression that came over her face ... it was glorious.

Her lips parted on a silent scream. Her eyes widened and then squeezed shut just before she threw her head back and I felt the gush of her reaching peak over my hand and lips. I sucked it all down, closing my own eyes and relishing in her first orgasm. When I was done and she was trembling with exhaustion beneath me—and only then—did I finally remove my fingers from her pussy and rear back to undo the front placket of my trousers.

Reaching up, I undid the strip of fabric binding her hands. Her limbs were lax and slender in my grip. I chuckled as she moaned lightly while I positioned her over my lap, lifting her slightly so that I could fit her opening at the tip of my cock.

"Ready?" I asked.

She didn't answer—at least, not in words. Instead, she lifted her head, cupped the back of my neck and pressed her mouth over mine. I took that to mean she was and I let her sink slowly upon my rod. More of her squirming made me nearly shoot my load in her, I clenched my teeth as I pulled away from her kiss. Pressing my face into her throat, I found the barrier of her virginity and sank further inside. There was no hiccup, no quick inhale of pain. Her insides squeezed me impossibly tight. A few quick pumps and I knew I'd be gone. Yet, I couldn't seem to help myself.

I'd sank fully into her and then, using my grip on her waist, I lifted her and thrust inside again and again and again, until I felt a tingle at the base of my spine rip through me. Pleasure raced into my mind and a split second later, I came, unleashing a torrent of my cum inside her. I pulled back a moment later, looking down at her half hooded eyes.

"I thought you said you couldn't take someone's pain away..." she muttered absently.

"I can't," I said.

She smiled. "Funny ... it didn't hurt at all."

Oh yes, this little Changeling was very dangerous indeed.

CHAPTER 12
CRESS

There was a certain languidness that I had only ever felt a few times before, usually after sunning myself until I almost burnt to a crisp on top of the convent storehouse. I'd never felt this way in the dark before, but it was luxurious. It made me realize that the nuns were probably so uptight because they'd never had an orgasm as good as the two Orion just gave me. I mean, seriously, the world could always benefit from more orgasms. They should be the currency of life. You want to buy some food? Get an orgasm. You want to solve an argument? Orgasm. Are you angry? Orgasm. Sad? Orgasm. It literally fixed every known problem.

Part of me was still freaking out that I'd just slept with, and thereby given my virginity to, someone who was essentially a stranger, but most of me just felt relieved that I didn't have that imaginary sign pointing at me anymore saying 'Here stands a Virgin.' I had always been more interested in sex than any of the other orphans at the convent—far too much for the nuns' self-preservation, but this ... if I had the energy to whistle, I would've. I mean *dear Gods*, Orion knew how to work that thing between his legs ... and his fingers ... and his mouth.

If I had been allowed to go to town more than once a year, I may have even experimented before now, but it was like the nuns had wanted to keep me prisoner, were scared of what would happen if they let me loose on an unsuspecting world. *Why*? I wondered absently. Because sex, I'd suddenly discovered, was the absolute best thing in the world.

Ha! If only they could see me now, naked in a conservatory with a strange Fae who looked more dangerous than anyone I'd met my whole life—he certainly had enough scars to deter the average person. I rolled to face him and lifted my head to settle it into my palm as I braced my elbow on the cushioned floor. "So," I started, "do I still smell human?"

Orion shook his head. "Your scent has been overwhelmed."

"Yeah, it has," I snorted. "But just to be sure..." I batted my eyelashes and reached for his arm. "I think I might need to get some more Fae scent on me—just in case. You know, for safety's sake."

Orion chuckled, deep and throaty, sending a shiver down my spine, before rolling on top of me. He pushed me onto my back and leaned over me to run his nose along one of my outstretched arms until he switched direction and headed for my upper chest, stopping just over my heart and breast. By the time he was done with the feather light touches, I was panting and arching my back, pressing myself against him once more. By Coreliath's beard, I wanted to feel him inside me again.

"Have an appetite for it now, do you?" Orion asked with a knowing smile.

"I mean, I could go for round two, if you're interested," I said with a nonchalant shrug. "I mean, if it's necessary—we should, definitely." I kept my face straight—or as straight as possible. All business. *One thousand percent ... just ... business,* I thought as my hands wandered down over his skin. We both knew that he had awoken a hunger in me that would not be easily sated.

"I would if I could, sweet Changeling, but if I do not return you to Court soon, then Roan and Sorrell will come and find us." He paused, lifting a brow as he looked down at me. "Unless you'd like that?" he inquired, keeping his expression even. At first, I thought he was joking, but the longer he stared at me the more I realized that he was serious.

"Stop messing around," I replied, my voice coming out more breathy than I had intended. The idea of the three of them doing the same things that Orion had done ... together ... at the same time. Them. And me. Me. And them. Them worshipping at the altar of my body. It was absurd, but it wasn't *un*appealing—I mean, if a girl liked that kind of thing. Which I might. Wouldn't know unless I tried.

"I'm not." Orion pushed to a sitting position and even half tousled, he looked gorgeous. His muscles bunched beneath his skin were displayed beautifully. Was there even a smidge of fat on him? If so, I hadn't been able to find it in all the time we'd been intertwined. "If you would like to explore your sexuality, then we'd be more than happy to help you. Fae are sexual creatures by nature; you saw from that small display between Roan and Ariana. Most of our celebrations involve a coalition of appetites or at least a party where everyone leaves with at least one partner. The fact that you remained untouched in the human world shows a strength of will I doubt many in our Court possess. I know some of it may not have been your choice since you were sequestered, but most Fae require physicality to access their abilities. It's a wonder you lived for as long as you did without acting on your sexual needs."

"It wasn't like I didn't think about it," I said defensively. "I was just never given the opportunity." Unless you counted the old men who'd come by the convent. "And the nuns weren't exactly forthcoming with information about it."

"There is nothing to be ashamed of in enjoying sex. I gave you pleasure, you gave me pleasure. We enjoyed ourselves, or at least I hope you did?"

I nodded vigorously. "Oh yes," I said quickly. "Definitely enjoyable. The most enjoyable experience of my life—so far."

He grinned, the stretch of his lips lighting up his face in a way that made him ten times as handsome. "Then there's nothing to worry about."

I couldn't help but return his smile. It felt like a weight had been lifted from my shoulders. My chest seemed to expand with breath more easily than it had done for most of my adult life.

"Come on," Orion said as he stood and offered me his hand, his gloriously naked form completely on display.

I bit my lip as I let him help me stand before swiping my dress up from the ground. "Can you help me put this back on? I've never worn anything like it before. The nuns would be scandalized," I said with a chuckle.

Orion's deft fingers had the straps in place with only a minimum of teasing before he dressed himself. Honestly, I was a little sad when he tucked his cock away. I hadn't had a chance to study one before and now that this whole new world had opened up to me, I couldn't deny that I was curious and excited. I wanted more of whatever he'd just given me. I wanted to know what I could do that would make him lose control just as much as I had. But right now, unfortunately, we had other things to focus on.

"Why is it so important that I'm a Changeling?" I asked as we worked our way back down the stairs to the main section of Orion's bedroom.

He paused at the bottom, turning as I stopped as well. His shoulders ratcheted up with tension and I watched the play of confused emotions cross his expression as he tried to come up with a response. After several moments of awkward silence and uncomfortable waiting, I sighed.

"Please don't lie to me," I said. "If you don't want to tell me, that's fine, I'll figure it out eventually—but just don't lie." There was nothing I hated more than I liar, which was probably why I butted heads with some of the nuns so much. It was ironic considering I was in the middle of lying my ass off, but that was to save my life. The nuns though ... they may not outright lie, but they deceived and lied by omission which to me was the same thing.

Orion faced me completely as I stood on the bottom step. We were almost eye level with one another. His scars and beautiful raven's black hair combined with his night sky eyes had me captured and in his control once more, even though I knew that wasn't really the case. Still, if he had asked me to jump in that moment, I would have ... onto him. "I think it's better if one of the others tells you; they know the history better than I do. I just have a good sense of smell, and you, pretty little Changeling, smell like you belong here," he said, lifting my hand and kissing the back of my knuckles.

"I do?" I whispered, my breath catching in my throat.

He nodded. "You smell like an old faction of the Fae

Courts that hasn't been seen in years, but again, I don't know the history very well. I was a mere babe when it all happened."

I nodded and let him lead me out of the room. I followed him through the hallways, my footsteps grazing lightly over the stones as I fixated on Orion, letting myself fall into a rhythm that matched his. I hadn't even realized where he'd been leading me until we were back in the banquet area—the throne room.

While I might have expected that the other two Fae —Sorrell and Roan—to be waiting to hear about how it'd all gone down—the loss of my virginity—that wasn't the case. Instead, it appeared as if all the other Fae living within the castle walls had suddenly been called to the room. The noise reached me first, and as we turned and entered the room, Orion's hand drifted to the small of my back to guide me through as I glanced around.

More tables had been added in the time we'd been away. Several long, elegant benches hosting creatures that were far more beautiful and elegant than any figure I'd ever seen before. Orion steered me to a table furthest from the doorway, where Roan and Sorrell were sitting along with a few others.

Roan caught my eye, a knowing smirk curving one side of his delectable lips. Sorrell's icy gaze met mine and his head tipped ever so slightly in what I was going to take as a nod of greeting. I could feel unfamiliar eyes land on me as we made our way around the table and took our seats. Ice skated down my spine and my skin lit with a burning feeling of discomfort. Sensations of all different kinds bombarded me. Was I losing my mind? Or was someone doing this to me?

The table we sat at was a large wooden circle with plates piled high with food in the middle. I watched as several of the others gathered at the table took a few of the pastries from the larger plates and felt my stomach rumble to life. I snatched a roll and stuffed it in my mouth as soon as I was situated. It ballooned my cheeks at the same time as the delicious taste of buttery freshness hit my tongue. I chewed and swallowed, already reaching for another, when a little buzzing figure entered my vision. A pixie, loaded down with a tray filled with empty and dirty plates flitted from the room. A kernel of guilt rose forth and I resolved to tuck something away to give to them later.

"Changeling," Roan said in greeting, drawing everyone's attention as Orion sat next to me.

The other Fae sitting at the table looked up with big curious eyes. A few leaned over and whispered to their neighbors in a tone so low I couldn't hear. It made me feel like a very small bug. The woman from earlier, Ariana, pursed her lips and shot a glare my way as her friend from the baths earlier, just stared longingly at Sorrell. If I was recalling correctly, she'd been complaining about their earlier ... session together and now she looked ready to do it all over again and right here, if he so much as looked her way. He didn't, though. Sorrell didn't let his gaze stray from me. Not even once.

"Roan," I replied, causing a gasp to go up from the others at our table and the tables around us.

"You may address me as Lord Carmine," Roan said coolly.

Yeah, fat chance, I thought. People had names for a reason and even with the sisters, I hadn't been much for using fancy titles. "Whatever you say, Roan," I replied, popping a chunk of those delicious rolls into my mouth.

A splotch of red formed over Roan's neck and spread upward and outward. It looked like that one time Nellie had walked into a patch of poisoned leaves that grew near the storage house. It had made her skin a fiery red for a fortnight and had itched like nothing she'd ever felt before, she'd said.

"That's a pretty color you're turning, *Lord Carmine*," I said, emphasizing his ridiculous title.

"Lord Chalcedony, would you mind introducing our guest this evening?" Roan said, nodding to Sorrell. They sounded so fancy now. I preferred them as just Roan, Sorrell, and Orion—though I couldn't help but wonder what Orion's last name was and if it was as fancy as the others.

"Are you sure that Orion doesn't want that pleasure? After all, he has tasted the Changeling," Sorrell said, his eyes on me as if he sought some sort of outward sign of my embarrassment. I didn't even blink. I'd taken the conversation I had with Orion to heart and if they really were as sexually open as he claimed, which—judging from some of the sounds coming from the corners of the room—didn't seem to be an exaggeration, then why should I feel shame just because I'd been raised differently.

I took the slight embarrassment I was feeling and shoved it into a mental box where Sorrell and Roan couldn't get to it and then shoved another roll in my mouth. I waited until I'd quietly chewed and swallowed the delicious offering before replying. "He does do wonderful things with his tongue," I commented lightly. "Things I didn't think possible." My voice sounded husky and filled with need, as though I couldn't wait to experience it again, which was true. I honestly couldn't wait to do all of that again. Soon. Preferably with him lying on his back and me sitting on his handsome face. I felt my groin tighten with the mental image that'd drawn.

Sorrell's face went carefully blank as his eyes traveled down the front of my body. Roan's expression darkened as the red splotches worked their way up his jawline. Orion choked, nearly spitting out the mouthful of whatever it was he'd been drinking. The orangish-gold liquid looked like nothing I'd ever seen before, but then that seemed to be the way of the Fae. Everything that they had was new to my eyes.

"May I ask what this drink is?" I asked, raising the glass in front of me with the orange-gold liquid.

"Fae wine. It packs a punch if you're not used to it so be careful," Orion said quietly as Sorrell got up and the temperature in the room dropped significantly until I could see my breath —and everyone else's—like clouds of fog. Quickly enough the room became quiet and as I looked around from my seat I saw that most of the Fae in attendance were turning to watch Sorrell.

"Friends, we have a guest in our midst tonight, someone who arrived unexpectedly, but the surprise was worth it. Cress, please stand," Sorrell said, raising his hand in my direction. I complied but shot him a glare as I did so, and I could swear I saw his mouth twitch with a grin before his face smoothed out once again. As I stood he twirled his finger in a circle and I followed his directions, spinning so I faced the majority of the Fae in attendance. "Cress is a Changeling that found her way to the castle when we landed. Of course, we couldn't turn her away, so she is staying with our Court until we can conduct the appropriate tests to discover her parentage, and where she belongs. I hope you all will be welcoming to our new arrival and be aware that she is unfamiliar with Fae customs."

As Sorrell spoke, the temperature surrounding me began to drop. All of the warmth was leached away from me until I felt the need to cross my arms over my chest, feeling how my nipples had grown so painfully hard that I felt as if they could practically tear a hole through the strips of fabric covering me. I shivered on the spot and when he finished speaking, I sank back into my chair, surprised to find it warm and the air temperature around it vastly different than where I had been standing a moment ago. *What in Coreliath's beard was that about?*

"Looks like someone likes being the center of attention," Ariana said from across the table. Several Fae around the table that had yet to be introduced to me snickered.

"And I'm sure you wore a sheer dress because you're such a wallflower," I replied testily before I could stop myself. The thing she wore could hardly pass for a dress. It was practically see through, her tits on full display for the whole world to see.

She gasped and turned to Roan. "Are you going to let a Changeling talk to me like that, my Lord?"

"Lady Ariana, if you can't handle it then you shouldn't start it. If it helps, I do find your dress this evening quite ravishing." He paused, lifting his brow as he smirked and looked downward—or more specifically, at her abundant bosom. She smiled back for a brief moment, arching her spine so that the curves of her breasts were thrust out and even more eye-catching. He continued a second later. "It probably seems strange to our guest."

Irritation spiked through me. I glanced down at my own breasts. Sure they weren't the size of melons, but they were alright. They were noticeable, at least. I frowned, glancing up at Orion from beneath my lashes. He'd seemed to like them just fine. Why did Ariana seem so intent on getting Roan's praise? Were all female Fae like that with these three? Would that be expected of me? I reached forward and snagged another pastry, this one filled with some sort of cream. Maybe that's what women did in the Fae Courts, but I certainly wasn't about to fall all over myself just to get their undivided attention, and if any of them expected me to be then they would be sorely disappointed.

As soon as I'd finished my pastry, pixies appeared out of the corners of the room—flocking together as they began carting away dishes before I'd even had a chance to try anything more. I pouted, but a moment later, new dishes were brought out. As they set down the new plates, I watched with fascination as the three lords served themselves, setting aside the choicest bits. I stared hard when Orion picked up a very interesting looking fruit. I noticed, too, that none of the other Fae even approached the new plates of food until the three princes had selected their bits. Pixies darted out in front of each of them and I watched as each prince held up a bite of food and let the little creatures nibble at whatever they held in their hands.

I expected them to be smacked away or yelled at but none of the lords responded at all, simply watching the pixie until it nodded, at which point they began eating their food.

"Why did you let them bite your food?" I asked quietly, leaning closer to Orion.

"They are poison testers," he replied, keeping his voice low so the conversation remained between the two of us.

"People try to poison you?" I gasped.

Orion nodded. "In this Court, we are royalty. The three of us are the pillars of the castle's magic. There are those who would try and steal our power and positions simply for the status it would offer them, although most would be incapable of controlling it. We have had many attempts on our lives over the years, some obvious, some not so much. Our parents instituted a rule that there are always at least a dozen pixies trained for tasting poison at any one time. Poison meant for Fae does not affect them as prevalently."

"I'm glad you survived," I replied, my voice barely above a whisper.

"Awww, is the Changeling sweet on you since you took her virginity?" Ariana asked loudly from across the table. Oppressive silence followed. She succeeded where others had failed. Embarrassment lit my face, heating my skin until I felt emblazoned.

Instead of letting that embarrassment keep me silent, however, it came out in fiery anger. My lips parted as murmurs began to fly through the hall. Orion's expression shut down—as did Sorrell's and Roan's. The three of them grew quiet in a way that reminded me of the absence of sound right before a giant thunderstorm.

"Perhaps I am," I snapped, sitting up straighter. I met Ariana's gaze and held it. "I understand being a virgin is practically unheard of in Fae Courts—but I wasn't raised with the Fae. Less than a day ago, I had never even met one."

"Well, I'm sure you weren't hard to please then," Ariana replied with a lifted brow.

A low growl emitted from Orion, but before he

could say anything, I spoke again. "You seem to be really interested in what I do with Orion," I said. "I wonder why that is."

"Lord Evenfall," Orion muttered.

"I mean, what I do with *Lord Evenfall*," I said loudly before anyone could be offended on his behalf.

Ariana glared at me, but her silence spoke volumes. Ergo—she didn't have a response. The rest of the table soon lost interest as more and more people dug into their food. Orion became quiet at my side. He didn't even comment when I snagged the fruit from his plate that I'd had my eye on. I bit into it, the whole thing bursting with flavor on my tongue that left me moaning and consuming the rest of it in wet, sticky bites. Several eyes lifted and watched as I did so, but no one said a word.

As I continued to snag food from the available plates as well as from Orion's platter, I watched as several different Fae in various colors of gowns—from deep forest green to bright sparkling blue—approached the table to speak with Roan and Sorrell. Interestingly enough, no one spoke with Orion, though they nodded his way in polite acknowledgment, and I wondered why that was. No matter who was talking, though, their gazes would inevitably travel over to me, skirting down in a sometimes curious glance or hostile glare until they'd satisfied their curiosity before leaving the hall to go and do whatever it was Fae did when not stuffing their faces.

Ariana stood, floated around the table and stopped

to run her fingers over Roan's shoulders in a slow, seductive glide. Her head lifted and her eyes zeroed in on me as she leaned down and pressed her breasts against him, marking her territory with a kiss to his cheek and a whisper against his ear before standing straight and moving back. As she passed me, she murmured, "Keep eating like that and no one will want to explore your desires with you, Switch."

"Switch?" I asked, but she was already gone.

The storm clouds were back on Orion's face and pity swam in the depths of his night sky eyes as he glared after her while absently answering me. "It's an insult for Changelings. Along the lines of your parents didn't even want you so they switched you for a human, which to us is about as low as it can get." His voice sounded like thunder in the distance and while part of me was screaming that I should be scared of him, all I wanted to do was climb him like a damn tree.

"I see," I replied, letting him know that I understood. I couldn't deny that the comment stung, but I'd been called worse by the nuns, so it wasn't anything new.

"Come," Orion said, standing and offering me his hand as he finally pulled his gaze away from where Ariana had exited and looked at me. "I'll give you a tour of the castle and we'll meet up with the others later to discuss your tests." I nodded, taking his hand and rising from my seat, snagging two rolls and squishing them in my free palm so the others wouldn't see. Hopefully, I'd be able to drop them for the pixies later. "Roan. Sorrell," Orion called as he stepped back, pulling me with him. The other two lifted their heads, nodding our way before returning to whatever conversations they'd been having among themselves.

I followed Orion out of the room, happy to be away from the peering eyes and muttered remarks of the other Fae. *Who knew that ignoring petty commentary from uptight Fae for the duration of a meal would be so tiring?* It was even a little more concerning, though, that these people really thought I was some sort of Changeling.

To be fair, I'd never really thought I'd belonged in the convent and I'd certainly been told how odd I'd been by everyone, but a Changeling? A lost Fae? Me? I snorted silently to myself. But if these guys thought I was a Fae, who was I to say they were wrong? Especially if telling them they were wrong would most assuredly land me on an executioner's block. I was willing to do whatever it took to avoid that. So, all that was left was for me to pass these tests and show them that I belonged here.

That didn't sound too hard ... right?

CHAPTER 13
SORRELL

Anger coated my vision, layering the room in a cool hue of blue frost. I could feel my skin grow cold and my breath puff out in a little white cloud in front of my face. The woman to my right shivered as my power stretched outward, reaching—seeking the warmth of others to suck it inside and freeze it over.

"L-Lord Ch-Chalcedony?" The woman spoke when I suddenly stood up as soon as Orion had taken the Changeling from the room. With her bright golden eyes and her even paler hair, she was a beauty. But the real irritation lay in her mouth. Every time, it seemed, she parted those pink lips of hers something rebellious was said.

"I'm going to the library," I said to Roan, ignoring the woman's faint call.

Victoria—one of my many bed partners—stood from across the table. "I'll attend to you, my Lord," she offered.

I held up a hand, staying her. "No," I said. "I wish to be alone." I didn't leave her much room for argument. Roan gave a nod of his understanding and I turned, striding from the room with quick, sure steps.

The library was my sanctuary. When I came to the double doors, I pushed through, turning and slamming them closed at my back, startling Groffet into dumping a stack of books he'd been putting back after my morning study session. "Lord Chalcedony!" he piped up, shock evident in both his tone and on his face as his big, bushy gray brows shot up, nearly disappearing beneath the green cap he wore.

The old dwarf ambled down the small ladder he had propped against the bookcase he'd been reshelving books on. I strode by, barely sparing him a glance as I headed to my desk where it was situated on the second platform in the center of the octagonal room.

"You're back early," Groffet commented.

I shot him a look of irritation that made it plain that I didn't want to talk about why that was, but as Groffet was as old as the Fae Courts themselves—he wasn't particularly put off by my glare or by the way the room dropped in temperature. Dwarves were few and far between and almost always immune to powerful Fae. They were like nature's neutral creatures. They were neither as powerful as Fae nor as weak as humans. They lived for hundreds of years, rarely contracting disease but held little magic. The one great thing they were known for was their stoutness and knowledge.

Giving up on ignoring the library's caretaker, I decided to question him for information. Perhaps he would know something about how to test a Changeling. "Groffet," I started as I stopped in front of my desk, turning and crossing my arms over my chest. "What can you tell me about Changelings?"

Groffet grunted as he shoved a stack of books onto a nearby table, the stack nearly higher than his head. "Well," he said, "I can tell you that there hasn't been one in several decades. The practice of switching Fae children for defective human ones has not been well received for centuries. The last Court to participate in such a practice was—"

"The Brightling Court, I know," I said. "What else can you tell me aside from the fact that they were the last Court to practice it?"

He nodded, his fat, grubby fingers coming up to stroke his full beard. The hair stretched from his face to halfway down his barrel chest. "Are you aware of the purpose of Changelings?" he asked.

I shook my head. "I didn't realize there was a point to it," I said. "I thought the whole issue with it was that it had no true purpose."

"There is always a purpose to old customs, my boy." Groffet waddled around the side of the table and across the floor, making his way to a section of books piled so high that even as tall as I was and standing on the platform, he disappeared from my view. "Old customs," he grunted from beyond the stacks, "are often set to maintain magical connection. Humans—although weak and without magic—come from nature. Their connection is to the land, itself, whereas Fae's connection comes from the Gods."

The tip of his pointed green cap appeared and I stared at it, watching it bob up and down as he did whatever he did out of my sight. "So, what was the purpose of trading Fae children for humans and subjecting Fae to spend years with the beasts?" I asked sharply.

Groffet chuckled, the sound dry and rather grating. I gritted my teeth to keep from using my usual commands on him. Unlike the others of our Court, Groffet wasn't just another subject. He was a pillar of our Court and the old creature knew it. He knew that I had no true power over him. Not unless I wished to speak with one of the head Courts. I pinched the bridge of my nose as I blew out a breath. Doing that would cause far more headache than I was willing to experience.

"Humans have their strengths," Groffet finally said, his voice slightly muffled. "The Brightling Court had their reasons for practicing in the Changeling switch. As you're aware, they were far more sympathetic to humankind's plight than any other Court."

"Yes, and look where that got them," I said, turning and uncrossing my arms as I circled my desk to take a seat. I pulled a book out of a pile to my right and flipped it open. On a single yellowed page was the list of all known Fae Courts and the one black mark, the one in which someone who'd had the volume before me had burned a line through that of the Brightling Court's name. "Humans are nothing if not treacherous."

"Humans are complex." I jumped and scowled when Groffet appeared in front of me, his fat, red nose peeking over the lip of my desk. He lifted up on his toes, placing a book on the edge of the workspace and shoving it until it rested flat. "This is an account of all things to do with Changelings," he said. "It should have some ideas as to tests you can perform on an individual to assess whether or not they are Fae."

"Can we determine which Court they would be from if they are a Changeling?" I asked.

Groffet backed away with a shrug. "You'll know when the Changeling's powers begin to show—as you know, each Court has a specific signature so to speak. For Prince Roan, it's fire and blood. For you, ice. And for Prince Orion—"

I waved my hand. "I'm aware," I snapped.

Groffet continued. "Among humans, without proper training and encouragement, their powers would've been weak. Around their own kind, they may experience some extreme shifts."

"Extreme shifts how?" I asked with narrowed eyes.

"Won't know until it happens," he said. "It changes per person. You have to understand that Changelings are creatures that are neither human nor Fae, yet they are both. Raised in one world, born from another.

Being switched so suddenly will make them experience a lot of changes in a very short span of time. They might experience rapid mood swings. It's recommended that Changelings bond to a person of one Court when in their training period. Unlike you and the rest of your Court, who have all had years to understand your magic and who you are, they've had absolutely no time."

I grabbed the book he'd placed on my desk and flipped it open, scanning the pages. My eyes widened. "These are tests?" I asked.

He nodded. "Says it right there on the book, doesn't it?"

Cocky little bastard, I thought, returning my attention to the book. "She's already engaged in sexual activity with a Court member," I said, the words scraping from my throat as I'd recalled the way Orion had taken her from the banquet. It was clear she'd enjoyed her time with him. I was not usually one to limit someone's sexual appetites, and I had no doubt he would have her again before the day was through, but she had come from the human realm. Orion was so rarely with female company, sometimes by his own choice—but more often than not by the ostracism of his beliefs and kindness towards the humans as well as the scars that littered his body. I wondered, briefly, if the Changeling had sensed that about him. Whereas Roan and I understood that humans could not be trusted as they were all deceptive and disloyal, time on the battlefields south of the human kingdom had made Orion particularly sympathetic towards them.

I shook my head. I would not let another brother in arms in this war against humanity fall victim to one of their plots, I decided. I would find out if the female was a Changeling and if she wasn't, I'd kill her myself if that's what it took. I slammed the book closed and stood abruptly.

"Find what you're looking for, Prince Sorrell?" Groffet asked with an arched brow.

I scowled, picking up the tome and tucking it under my arm. "I will be in my chambers," I said. "Make sure I'm not disturbed."

"Of course." He bowed as I passed, but I was not fooled. He did so only out of marginal respect—not for me, but for my home Court. The Court of Frost was one of the most powerful in the land and I was the second heir.

CHAPTER 14
ROAN

I groaned as I rolled off the willing body beneath me. My chest pumped up and down. Sweat coated every inch of my skin. Ariana turned and cuddled up against me and I allowed it for a moment. Then, as always, it grew annoying. I withdrew my arm from under her back and waved to the sheer robe waiting for her on the back of my desk chair. With a sigh and an eye roll, she crawled out of my bed and reached for the robe.

"I would have thought you'd be used to sleeping with another body near by now," she said tightly.

I sat up, stretching my arms as I pushed them behind my head, propping my neck at an angle as I watched her stride through the room and find the remainder of the dress I'd ripped from her as soon as I'd gotten her alone in my chambers. "Maybe another time," I offered with a playful smirk.

She shot me a look. We both knew the truth. There

would never be a time that I'd allow a woman to sleep alongside me. Not since my ex-fiancée had nearly carved my heart from my chest in a bid to claim my position of power over my own Court.

"Have you given much thought to my proposal from last time?" she asked, lifting the long silky strands of her hair out of the back of her robe and quickly braiding it down the side of her breast. I watched the mundane task, wondering if I continued to return to Ariana out of true pleasure or out of a sense of routine.

"I have," I said blandly.

Her head jerked up and her eyes blazed with excitement. "And?" she prompted.

I stretched again, turning and swinging my legs over the side of the bed before standing up. "The Court of Crimson does not need another member."

As expected, Ariana's exuberant expression soured. Her arms clamped beneath her buxom chest, lifting the soft mounds I'd just granted more than an hour of attention—*each*. "You will have to announce a new fiancée soon, Roan—" I cut her a look so dark that she snapped her mouth shut and her eyes moved to the ground as she corrected herself. "Lord Carmine."

Strangely enough, I hadn't done the same to the little Changeling now attached to Orion's side. Hearing my given name from her lips had been ... almost refreshing. From Ariana, however, it was an insult to refer to me with such informality. She might have been my regular bed partner but she was nothing but a warm body to help restore my magic, someone to pass the time with. I would not marry her.

"The answer is no," I said. "I have been granted all the time I would desire in choosing a new fiancée." Within reason, my mother had stated, but there was no need to specify that part to Ariana.

Ariana stiffened her spine. "Of course, my Lord." She bowed briefly. "May I be excused?"

I waved her away as I found my trousers and pulled them up my legs. A moment later, I was alone. I found myself moving to the window and staring out over the vast space we now inhabited. Before, we'd been stationed in the Eastern quadrant—just outside of the human kingdom's border. Now, we were inside, to the north. We were not at all where we were supposed to be.

I looked down and clenched my fist. I called my magic to me, felt sweat bead on my brow and the air around me crackle with energy as I conjured a ball of flame in my palm. It flared to life and dispersed, causing me to turn away from the window with a curse. What a disappointment we were as a Court.

Oh yes, the others and I held sway—we held our power and position—but we were only three. It took, on average, *four* royals to power a monstrosity such as a Fae castle. Perhaps the elders had thought that with our lineages—Sorrell, Orion, and I could handle it, and for a time, we had. But after Franchesca's betrayal and Orion's continued wounds in battle, we were running dry. Add a Changeling into the mix and we were well and truly fucked.

I moved to my desk and lifted a letter that had appeared, tucked just inside of the portal alongside my bed where it always did. I hoped when I read it that it'd be good news. I tore the crimson seal and flattened the parchment, leaning over the desk as my eyes read over the black script in my mother's handwriting. I breathed a sigh of relief as I scanned the words.

She was giving us time. A reprieve that we all sorely needed. Dealing with Fae Court politics, the war with the humans, and a Changeling? We were already stretched too thin as it was. All the elders had managed to do in placing the three of us in charge of this Court had been to sow the seeds of our inevitable failure. We now had a fortnight before Sorrell, Orion, and I needed to have the castle moved into position. It wasn't much, but it was something.

Once I was done reading the letter, I lifted it up and conjured another ball of fire. The parchment lit up in my palm and was burned away until only ash remained. Two weeks to deal with the Changeling. Two weeks to restore our magical reserves. Hopefully, by then we'd be prepared enough for the impending siege we were tasked with.

By the Gods, we had better be ready.

CHAPTER 15
CRESS

Apparently, when Orion had offered to take me on a tour of the castle, what he really meant was a tour of his bedroom ... again. I'm sure he meant to take me on a tour, but there was something electric moving between us. As we left the banquet hall, a few heated glances and the brush of his fingertips against my arm was all it had taken. We'd barely made it in the door of his tower room before his lips were crashing against mine. We'd replayed and expanded on the events from earlier.

My body collapsed against his several hours later and as a yawn stretched my jaw, I finally let myself cave in to the exhaustion the last day had left in me. Almost as soon as I surrendered to sleep, however, a new anxiety sprang forth.

My dreams weren't usually anything exciting or terribly surprising. They were the same kinds of dreams that I'd heard several of the orphans at the convent talk about. I was often falling down long dark tunnels or searching for something that I could never find in dense forests that were too smoky to navigate.

Shocking, I know, someone who was abandoned searching for something in their dreams. Like perhaps ... birth parents?

But this dream was different. In this dream, I was flying—soaring through the air. I dipped and weaved, using great golden wings that looked as if they belonged on a dragonfly to sail through the clouds. I lowered them, falling down several hundreds of feet until I found the tops of the trees. As I moved between the trees, the minds of the animals further below reached out and touched my own, greeting me as they might a familiar friend. Each time I climbed higher than the treetops I felt the frigid air slap against my cheeks, growing colder each time I tried to ascend again into the clouds, and ducked back down, taking shelter between the branches once more.

The farther I flew, the darker it seemed to get. The trees grew closer together, making it increasingly difficult to maneuver through them, their branches blocking out the light. Yet at the same time, the darker it grew amidst the branches, the clearer the ground below became. Just once, right before I dipped down below for the last time, I looked over my shoulder and saw the fire of a burning sun following me. It scared me, that sun.

My wings beat faster and what had originally been

friendly greetings from the animals were now pleas for help, screaming in my ears. They grew louder and louder, echoing in my mind. I couldn't stop, though; if I stopped, I knew the sun would catch up to me. I ignored the cries from the animals as I darted above the treetops, turning in a circle. An icy wind blew against me, shoving me back, forcing me down into the branches. It lashed against me, painful and sharp. I gasped for breath as a branch slapped me in the face. I turned again, panting, searching. I needed a way out. I couldn't stay down here. The darkness was preferable to the chasing sun, but something told me that I wasn't just being chased—I was being herded into the waiting darkness. The darkness wasn't scary, it was comforting.

I sucked in a breath and made my choice. I dove straight down, caving into the feelings and sliding as far into the darkness waiting below as I could. As soon as the treetops closed in, removing all of the sun's rays and the ice from above, a light burst forth from my body, breaking through the darkness. I gaped as my skin glowed to life, a golden hue emanating from me, chasing away the shadows even as I followed after them—trying to catch them before they could disappear entirely. Small dark smoky trails disappeared in my hands as I reached for them, capturing them just as they slipped through my fingers. I didn't want it to leave. I didn't want to be alone again, but it was already gone. The darkness having been chased away by something inside of me.

A scream of frustration erupted out of me, both in my dream and in real life, startling me awake as I bolted upright in bed. My heart was pounding and sweat dripped down my neck as my breath heaved in and out of my chest.

For a moment, I just blinked and tried to breathe. It took me several more moments before I remembered why I wasn't back in the bunk room at the Convent of Amnestia. I wasn't there because I'd left, I'd been led away—again, by something inside of me just like my dream—to this place. A Fae castle on the edge of the human kingdom of Amnestia. My whole life had changed.

I wiped sweat from the back of my neck and turned to the side, wondering if my scream had woken Orion, but he was gone. I frowned. The rumpled sheets were the only sign he had ever been there at all. Stretching and pushing out of the bed, I got up and paused when I glanced over a slip of parchment that had been left, neatly folded on an assortment of clothes waiting for me on a chair next to my side of the bed. I picked up the creamy, thick paper and opened it.

A dress for you for today. We will be in the library. Come and meet us when you're ready. Feel free to use the facilities and eat first. - O

Well, that answered one question at least, I thought. I considered going to the bathing chamber and washing before getting dressed but decided against it. I didn't want to run into any of the other Fae if I could help it.

As dinner last night had proven, I wasn't exactly a favorite of theirs.

I groaned when I finished dressing and turned to survey myself in the tall, oval mirror in the corner of Orion's bedroom. I should have known ... even though the material was thicker, it was still scandalous by human standards. The dress didn't so much have a slit up the side, as a side completely cut out of it up to the top of my hip, so that one need only push the material slightly, or possibly even walking too fast, and the wearer—which would be me—would be exposed. There was also a section cut from the opposite shoulder down to the hip where the slit came up. The material, itself, looked as if it were held together by little more than a tiny section of metal no larger than a fat coin. Some beading and a flower covered the area where the fabric connected and I couldn't help but wonder if it had been torn many times with the Fae's proclivity for sexual activities or if this was just how it was originally designed to be worn. It also made me wonder who these clothes belonged to.

With the dress on and my hair finger combed, I set off to the throne room since that seemed to double as a banquet room. *If that was where they kept the food then that was where I was going*, I decided as my stomach grumbled to life. I headed out, but after the third hallway I'd turned down, I stopped and looked around. I could've sworn this was the way to the banquet hall, but I should have already arrived. All of the hallways looked the same to me; there were only so many perfectly carved rock walls and fiery sconces I could look at before they all seemed to repeat themselves. Wait, *were* they repeating themselves? Had I been going in circles?

I had no clue what to do. Without any pixies or Fae in sight, I grimaced and turned, heading back the way I came. I'd just start from where I'd come from and hope I managed to figure it out from there. I followed my feet, as odd as that sounded, letting them lead me back through the odd twists and turns. My mind wandered and I let myself meander through the hallways until finally, as my stomach grumbled for the hundredth time, I stopped and stomped my foot in outrage. If they were going to have such a confusing castle, the least they could do was provide some sort of map.

Shoving my fingers through my short blonde hair and pulling in irritation as I let out another grunt of frustration, I looked to the empty walls and narrowed my eyes. "Hello?" I called. Nothing. "Pixies?" Surely the pixies wouldn't abandon me here. I fed those little bastards more than once. "If you help me out, I'll get you more Fae food," I offered aloud. I wasn't sure why they didn't eat the leftover food that the Fae didn't touch, but they constantly seemed to be starving and the few times I'd tossed them rolls or pastries they had been devoured in a matter of seconds.

A long corridor stretched in front of me and I was about to turn around when I felt this hum in my bones that made me want to move towards it. As I moved down the hallway, the hum only grew in its intensity until I stepped through an arch and the room opened up before me. A railing curled around a walkway that jutted out from the edges of the room, all of which hung above a giant spinning ball of strands of light. One was blue, one red, and one purple. As I continued to stare at it, the glass orb shuddered, vibrating with energy.

Inside the strands of light, there was something else. Another, smaller, orb. The second one looked as though it was made of all the elements and none, light and dark, fire and ice, lightning, but not the natural kind of lightning I'd seen strike the mountain during horrible thunderstorms that tore through the countryside in the summertime. I couldn't help but lean forward as I tried to get a closer look. As I did, the colors changed, distorted into one another so the flames that flickered across the surface occasionally morphed from the natural yellow and red to purples, blues, and greens.

It was like looking at all of creation and destruction. If I were to go back thousands of years and watch as the whole of our world was born, I might have seen something like this as it exploded—forming vast mountain ranges and valleys and plains and ... life. Life and death. Because there was no such thing as life without death. It was breathtaking. I might have stared at it forever if it wasn't for the footsteps that sounded down the hallway at my back.

I panicked. I didn't know if I was supposed to be here or not. Without a second thought, I backed up and pressed myself against the wall just by the door, hiding in the corner shadows as male voices flowed down the corridor. Hopefully, no one would be able to see me here.

"She needs to be tested. We can't just have a human milling around our Court harassing other Fae." Roan's voice was the first I could distinguish.

"She's a Changeling." That was Orion. "Not a human."

"We've established that with the fucking," Sorrell spoke—the third and final voice as they stopped just beyond the room, not yet entering but right there. So close. "Did you feel your magic replenish?" he asked.

Orion was quiet for a moment before speaking. "The Changeling was very responsive," he said. I waited for more, but after a moment when he hadn't spoken again, Sorrell responded.

"That doesn't answer my question," he said.

Someone sighed heavily. "I wasn't really paying attention," Orion answered. "During. I do feel stronger, though."

I cringed. *Wow*, I thought, *what a glowing review.* Then again, Orion wasn't the talker of the bunch.

"But do you feel stronger because of the girl or because you had sex?" Sorrell pressed.

"I don't know!" Orion snapped.

"Great," Roan said. "Shadow boy is too pussy sick to think straight."

"You're just mad that she didn't want to fuck you," Orion replied sharply.

"Enough!" Sorrell cut in. "There are other tests we can perform, but it will be tricky to get her to agree to it." He paused and I assumed there was some sort of silent exchange between the three of them. Maybe some eyebrow raising or swaggering. *Ugh, men.* These three gossiped and kept secrets worse than the women from the local villages. "We need to bombard her with enough magic to challenge her."

"But if she's not truly a Changeling, that might kill her," Orion said.

My eyes widened. *What was it with these Fae and trying to kill me? I mean, seriously, what did I ever do but break into their castle, eat their food, learn their secrets, sleep in their beds ...* I stopped and shook my head. Thinking about it really wasn't helping my case.

"If she's human," Sorrell repeated. "If you're so sure that she's a Changeling, then she should be fine. According to the book Groffet gave me, introducing her to high levels of powerful magic will trigger *her* magic. Fae who have not been taught or raised in the Courts often can't reach their magic for long stretches. If Fae children are not raised around magic, then they don't know how to actively recognize it. An adult Fae without magic is a liability. She needs magic if she's to survive the Courts. If she's human then, obviously, she will die, but she would be put to death anyway so it won't matter."

A cold lump formed in my stomach at Sorrell's words. What if this was all just a mistake? What if I really was human and Orion had just smelled something else on me? They were going to kill me. Maybe not intentionally, but they were going to do it. A shudder worked its way down my spine. Okay, I decided internally. It was time to cut and run. I needed to get out of here. How? I didn't know, but it needed to happen. Maybe I could talk the pixies into helping me, but first I needed to figure out what else they might be planning and then figure out a way to get out of this room without them knowing that I'd been listening.

"You want to risk killing a Changeling because a book that is centuries old says it works as a test to bring out her Fae powers?" Orion scoffed. At least he sounded offended by my potential death. Good to know that I'd chosen the one with a conscience to fuck me.

"Listen, just because you've got your cock wet for once doesn't mean I don't know what I'm talking about. Groffet and I did plenty of research and this is the fastest, most reliable test we could find."

"What harm could it do?" Roan asked.

"It could kill her, you idiots," Orion said, a growl in his tone.

"Then there's one less Changeling," Sorrell said dryly. "The last member of the Brightling Court is snuffed out like the rest of her Court. She's not supposed to exist anyway," he hissed, his voice cold and hard.

I swallowed and tried to steady my breathing, but I was getting dangerously close to full on panicking. I could feel sweat forming against my brow and sliding down the small of my back. My hands were damp.

"I'm not agreeing to anything until I see this book for myself," Orion said, his voice low and rough.

"Fine, come to my section of the library," Sorrell said, his words clipped and tight with irritation.

As their footsteps faded back down the hall, I allowed myself a few shaky breaths before I got myself back under control. I stepped into the corridor, moving quickly as I retraced my steps. When I was back in the main hallway, I called out again, "Pixies? Could someone lead me to the throne room? I'll give you some food when we get there if it's out."

This time a gaggle of pixies descended from the ceiling all seeming to jockey for position in front of me as they waved me forward to follow them. If I had any amusement left in my body to laugh, I might've, but I was far too concerned with the fact that the three Fae in charge of this Court were trying to kill me. I smiled at the buzzing pixies and let them lead me, pushing and shoving each other as they tried to get my attention—and the food I was offering at the end of our journey. I forced myself to relax, breathing in through my nose and releasing the air through my lips as we strode down the corridor.

I nodded to the pixies and whispered a promise to come back soon with food, as they led me straight to the entrance of the throne and banquet room. They nodded and disappeared back into the walls and ceilings as I leaned around the corner, peering into the large room as quietly as possible. As far as I could see, though, there was no one waiting for me. I ventured towards the closest table with food on it and grabbed a handful of rolls before tossing a few—snickering lightly as pixies shot back out of the walls and ceiling to snatch the food and buzz away as their tiny little sharp teeth ripped into the succulent pastries.

As I wandered around the different food laden tables I realized I'd never consistently liked the food the nuns made, although no one else seemed to have any issues with it, but I loved the food here. Was Fae food addicting for humans? If I escaped would I be able to find food this good again? The questions plagued me as I began to stuff my face with fruit, what I assumed were vegetable dishes, pastries, and anything else I could get my hands on. I even tried some of the Fae wine that Orion had warned me about. It was all delicious. And okay, maybe I was stuffing my face to comfort myself. Food made me feel better.

If I was going to escape and be on the run from potentially murderous Fae, then I needed to fuel up and that was something I'd never had the opportunity to do before. The pixies came and went, clearing plate after plate as I worked my way through all the different dishes, trying everything and having seconds of what I liked the most. By the time I was done, I was ready for a nap, my belly pleasantly full and my mind completely relaxed despite the thoughts of my imminent death. The food had done its job.

"By the Gods look at this one, gorged herself

stupid, she has," a rough feminine voice came from behind me, but I couldn't see who was speaking.

"She'll need it for what's coming, though. Dark times ahead, indeed," another, more masculine voice replied.

I wanted to turn and give whoever was speaking a piece of my mind, but I couldn't get my eyes to open, sleep had taken me too far down. It was only when someone shook my shoulder that I startled back to reality to find Orion's night sky eyes staring down at me.

"Feeling okay, Changeling?" he asked.

Back to Changeling, was it? Their conversation in the hallway replayed at hyper speed in my head. My mouth dried up, no words willing to make it past my lips, so instead, I just made a croaking sound.

"Here, have some water," he said as he handed me the glass that had been sitting to my right while I ate.

I gratefully accepted it and guzzled the contents, wetting my chapped lips and dry throat as though I hadn't had a drink in days.

"Better?" he asked.

"Much. Thank you," I said, feeling suddenly wary.

"Are you feeling okay? I left the note for you to meet us in the library, but when you didn't show up I came looking for you," he said, concern pinching his brows, but there was something off about his face, as though he was reading from a script.

"Fine, just ate too much and fell asleep."

"Would you like to see what we've found?" he asked, holding his hand out to me.

I stood and noticed his eyes rake over me even though he seemed to try and resist it at first. We walked out into the hall and towards what I assumed was the library where the others were waiting to kill me. Death by magic. At least it would be a fancy exit, not many people in this region could say they went out that way. I looked up at Orion, which was silly because I almost stumbled as we were walking, which made him stop and look at me. I felt something pushing inside me and then words came spilling out.

"Please don't kill me," I blurted, startling him. "Don't let them kill me. You have such good food, and I just started having sex, and that's fun, and it would be really awful if I couldn't do that again. And you have really pretty eyes and a nice chest, and an even better cock." My Gods, I couldn't seem to stop talking. "I really don't understand why people don't talk to you more when you're the nicest Fae I've ever met and really good in bed. I mean seriously the best—not that I've had a whole lot of experience, but do you really need experience to know what makes you feel good?" I couldn't stop. It just kept coming out. Word vomit. I clamped a hand over my mouth to stop myself from talking.

Orion's eyes went wide and his jaw dropped open for a moment before he visibly seemed to regain his composure and asked, "Why do you think we're going to kill you?"

I pressed my lips together and held my hand over them so I couldn't answer, but when Orion pried my fingers away my lips popped open and I said, "Because I found this big spiny orb thing that is all magic-y and makes me want to touch it, then I heard you talking about testing me with magic and if I'm human it will just kill me and I'm pretty sure I'm human. At least, I think I am. I've never had Fae powers—even when I was a kid. Seriously, why am I saying all this out loud? I can't stop!"

"Someone must have put a charm in your drink," he began and when I narrowed my eyes he quickly raised his hands defensively and added, "It wasn't me! It's a loose lips charm. It lowers the barrier between what the person is thinking and what they say, it also makes them more suggestible to ideas."

"Can we skip the library and have sex again?" The question popped out before I could even register that I was thinking it. I clamped my hand over my mouth again, pinning my lips in place.

Orion stared at me, his wide eyes watching me with concern and confusion. Then he laughed. Not just any laugh, but an uncontrollable one. He covered his mouth, but I heard the laughs as they escaped. He shook his head, turning away as he tried to get himself under control. It was so startling that it made me laugh too. I dropped my hand slowly and when he looked back at me, still stifling laughter, I couldn't help it anymore. A small chuckle turned into a laugh and then another and another, until the both of us were wiping tears from our eyes.

I paused when I looked back at his face and saw black streaks cascading down his cheeks. I dropped my hands and reached out towards him. He stilled, his laughter cutting off abruptly, as I brushed my thumb against his skin, swiping the tear from its path. I pulled my hand back and looked at the black liquid on my skin for a moment before it was oddly absorbed into me.

"What is this?" I asked.

"It's part of being a prince of the Night Court," he said quietly. "It's one of the reasons people stay away from me."

"Why?" I asked.

"The Night Court is..." He grimaced, cutting himself off. "It's difficult to explain and I'm not sure now is the right time for that."

"Well," I started, "I think you're sexy, and if they are turning away from you because of the color of your tears then that's their loss. I want you, Orion. I want to get to know you, learn about you and your past and what you want for the future if you'll let me and don't end up killing me when you bombard me with magic. Are you sure you don't want to have sex one last time?" I slapped my hand over my mouth again as my, apparently filthy, mind took a left turn from complimenting the man to trying to get him into bed. Again.

He chuckled softly, before he said, "I wouldn't let them do this if I didn't believe you were a Changeling.

You trusted me to make your first time good, trust me with this?"

I wanted to tell him there was a huge difference between making sex good and possibly dying, but I did trust him, all the way down to my toes, and that was what mattered, so I nodded. He took my hand once more and led me onward.

CHAPTER 16
CRESS

Orion led me to a great big room that looked as if it'd been taken straight from a storybook. The nuns at the convent had kept a few books here and there, but nothing so grand as this. I released him as I stumbled forward, standing in the middle of the room with my head craned back as I just turned and turned.

"These are all yours?" I asked, mouth agape.

He chuckled, but before he could respond, the doors opened and Sorrell and Roan appeared. They'd been talking quietly, their heads tilted down towards each other as if they were sharing secrets, but as soon as they looked up and saw me, their words cut off. *Wow,* I thought, *way to not hide the fact that they were talking about me. Who knew I could be so popular?*

"You found her," Sorrell said with a nod Orion's way.

"Was I lost?" I asked. Other than the look of irritation he shot me, he didn't respond to my question. Asshole.

"Where's Groffet?" Orion asked.

"He's doing his duties," Roan said.

I pursed my lips, but despite the fact that Orion nodded in understanding, neither of them gave me anything—not a look, not an explanation of who this Groffet was or what duties he was doing. It was like I was invisible. Lovely.

I headed for the desk towards the back and center of the library, clambering up onto the platform, my skirts tangling around my legs as I hefted my much smaller frame onto the small stage. "Hasn't anyone here heard of stairs?" I grumbled as I rolled and popped up to my feet.

Roan smirked as he strode forward without saying anything. He moved around the side of the platform. He waved his hand over a section of the floor and a set of small stairs leading up to the desk appeared—rising from the floor.

"Oh." I blinked down at it dumbly. Well then …

I scooted several stacks of books to the side and perched on the corner of the desk, folding my hands in my lap and adjusting myself so that all of my bits were covered before finally looking up and meeting their gazes. Sorrell looked as if he'd swallowed a particularly sour fruit. "Well," I started, "let's do this. Test me. Hit me with the magic. Wham. Bam. Magic me, man."

Sorrell walked past Roan and with a twist of his hand in the air, he made a spiral of blue sparks appear.

"Wait—" Orion held his hand out but it was too late. The blue sparks slammed into my chest, nearly knocking me off the desk.

I let out an *oomph* and sent a stack of books to the floor when I reached out and grabbed onto the edge of the desk, clutching it for all that I was worth as frost crept through my veins. A shiver skirted down my spine and when I breathed, cold clouds of air escaped from between my lips.

"I thought I said to wait!" Orion snapped as I managed to get myself under control. Other than a sharp and barely bearable cold wave that hit my system, it honestly wasn't that bad.

"We don't have time to wait, Orion," Sorrell replied coolly. "We need to ascertain if this girl is, in fact, a Changeling and if she is, if she's from the Brightling Court."

I huffed out a breath, inhaling and exhaling quickly as if doing so would make the cold go away faster. Gods, it was freezing. I put my hands to my arms and rubbed up and down rapidly, trying to get some warmth back into my limbs. When I looked up, Orion was standing in front of Sorrell, clutching his shirt in his hands that swirled with darkness. I shook my head, sure I was seeing things—but I wasn't. Dark tendrils seeped out of his skin, between his knuckles. Sorrell didn't even flinch as the curls reached up and stroked him with their magic.

"It's your turn," Sorrell said calmly.

"Orion," I called, sliding off of the desk onto shaky legs. "I-it's fine."

Orion's gaze snapped to mine and he cursed. "Your lips are turning blue," he growled.

I shrugged. "Ice man has that effect on people, I guess."

"Ice man?" Sorrell's white-blue eyes narrowed on me at the insult.

I arched a brow his way. "Problem?" I countered. I really wanted to punch him in his smug handsome face. Yeah, okay, I could admit he was handsome, but he was also an asshole. And if I knew how to punch then I totally would've done it. Punched him right in his nose.

"This is a fucking disaster," Orion said.

"If you won't do it, then I guess I'll have to take my turn," Roan announced. All heads turned his way and this time, I didn't even see it coming before a wave of fire stole through me, red coils of magic—crimson smoke—wrapped around me. It sucked all of the coldness away until nothing was left but a burning heat. Sweat poured down my spine. I fanned my face and stumbled away from the desk as I tried to get my dress off.

"What are you doing?" Orion rushed towards me.

"It's hot," I complained. It was more than hot, it was impossibly humid. Sweltering.

"Stop." He stayed my hands, holding my wrists. I squirmed, wrestling to get free of him. I needed my clothes off. I needed something to relieve the feel of fire boiling in my veins. Man, they hadn't been kidding about this magic nearly killing me. I felt like I was already dying from heatstroke or something. My lips and tongue were dry. My throat parched. I needed something to drink.

"Water," I croaked. "I need water."

Orion shook his head, his lips moving as he spoke, but whatever he said was lost to me. I couldn't hear anything but the rushing of blood in my veins—powering through my ears. The rush of it was like a mighty storm.

One more ... I just had one more magic to deal with. His. One more and this would all be over. I could feel his darkness reaching for me. When I looked down at where he clasped my wrists, I saw the tendrils curling around my fingers—brushing against my skin. It didn't hurt.

My skin looked strangely golden, as if it were glowing under all that darkness. Orion's eyes met mine. His lips parted. I didn't know what he was saying, but I nodded my head anyway—hoping he was asking for permission. Man, I really wanted to get this test over with. I was getting tired. My lids drooped as I slumped forward.

Orion caught me and cradled me against his chest. Over his shoulder, I saw Roan move closer—his red hair like a flame under the light of the room. His lips were turned down in a frown. I knew Sorrell was behind him, but I couldn't see that far back. Roan was enough. His eyes as they lifted and met mine were confused and ... almost apologetic. He hadn't seemed apologetic a moment ago when he'd shot me with his magic. I knew I'd asked for it and all that, but man, he could've at least warned me.

I stared at him, keeping my eyes on his as Orion's black magic swirled around me—around us. It rose up from his skin and burst outward until all that I saw was black. A dark oblivion. I was almost completely shrouded by darkness when something else crept forward—that fire from before. It wrapped around me, coiling tightly and shielded me from the dark gloom of Orion's magic. It clung to me, but this time, it wasn't burning. It was ... nice, actually. Really nice. I snuggled into it and felt my body being lifted and passed to someone else.

New arms closed around me, warm and safe. Strange. I'd never felt safe with anyone before. Not until Orion, but as these new limbs curled beneath my back and thighs, hoisting me against an equally warm chest, I realized I felt that now. I felt protected. Maybe I was crazy—it wouldn't have been the first time I thought that. Fae were supposed to be enemies of the human race—my own best friend had been terrified of them—but ever since arriving at this magical castle, I'd felt everything but afraid. I'd felt confused, angry, excited, irritated, and hungry, but never terrified. Not true fear. They didn't scare me, but if I was honest with myself, what they made me feel was far more dangerous. They made me feel almost ... secure.

CHAPTER 17
CRESS

I woke up with a headache. I tried to open my eyes and was met with a burning light. With a groan, I slammed them shut again and rolled over onto my side. My hands spread out. Without my sight, I had to feel out where I was. Covers—sheets softer than anything I'd ever felt—moved against my skin, sliding down to my waist as I hesitantly sat up.

It took several more minutes for me to even crack my eyelids open without feeling like a shard of pure sunlight was being stabbed through my skull. When I did, I surveyed my surroundings. It wasn't Orion's room, but it was a bedroom. I sat up and moved to the side, frowning down at my body. My clothes had been removed and I'd been changed. I should've felt violated, perhaps even angry, but honestly—whoever had dressed me had far better sense than the guys because no longer was I wearing a skimpy dress made of nothing. Instead, I was dressed in a man's shirt that hung down to my thighs and tight trousers that were obviously made for someone much taller. At least, it had to have been made for someone taller considering that the ends of each leg were bunched up several inches at my ankles and the waistband was above my belly button. At least they were comfortable, I decided as I stretched out a leg and then my other and hopped off the bed.

I looked back as I stood up and noticed that the bed, itself, was much larger than anything I'd ever seen. It was larger, even, than Orion's had been with dark red sheets tucked around the edges. The rest of the room was set to match as well. With deep burgundy curtains covering the windows and similarly colored drapes hanging from the ceiling. Paintings marred the surface of the stone walls. Depictions of beasts I'd never before seen—soaring through the skies, hunting through forests, swimming in deep oceans. Each was more detailed than the last. One beast was so lifelike that I could've sworn its fur was glistening and shifting with an invisible breeze blowing across it.

I reached out to see if it was when a voice stopped me. "I see you're awake."

I paused, my hand half raised—the itch to stroke the fur warring with my need to look over my shoulder. The second urge won out over the first as I sighed and turned around.

Roan stood in the doorway, his arms crossed over

his massive chest as he eyed me. "Did you paint this?" I asked, pointing to the image.

"I did." He dropped his arms and strode further into the room. I didn't flinch away as he walked right up to me, towering over me with his much larger frame. I just tilted my head back and looked up at him, waiting. "You're not afraid of me?" he asked.

"Should I be?"

He frowned, but instead of answering he asked another question. "Do you remember what happened?"

"I remember you hitting me with magic—all three of you—and then I remember passing out," I answered. "That's about it. What happened? I'm not dead, so I assume I passed the test."

His lips pressed together before he parted them again on a sigh. "You passed," he said, but it didn't sound like he was happy about that. "The results, however, were inconclusive."

"What does that mean?"

"It means that while you survived being bombarded with three different types of magic, we still weren't able to say if you're from the Brightling Court. You showed an affinity for a different type of magic."

"Which magic?" I asked. He leaned forward as if he wanted to touch me, his eyes scanning down my form. I shifted, frowning as my curiosity rose. "Roan?"

His lips twitched. "Why aren't you afraid?" I wasn't sure if he was asking me or if the question just slipped out. His eyes appeared unfocused. Even though he was looking straight at me, it felt like he was looking *through* me.

"I don't know," I answered anyway. "I guess you just don't seem that scary to me."

He hummed beneath his breath. The scent of spices and burning wood filled my nostrils. It was actually quite pleasant. It made me want to push my face forward and bury it in his chest—the source of the scent—and breathe it in as deeply as I could.

"You showed an affinity for the Court of Crimson's magic," he finally said after a beat of silence.

"Okay..." I didn't know what that meant.

"It's magic from *my* Court," he continued.

"What does that mean?" I pressed. I felt my body incline forward, slanting towards his. I couldn't seem to help it.

"It means, little Changeling," he started, reaching up and pinching my chin between his thumb and forefinger, "that you might actually be from my Court."

"Is that bad?" I asked.

He shook his head. "It's not bad so much as it's ... unexpected."

"Why unexpected?" I pulled myself back, removing my chin from his grasp as my brows lowered. "Do you think I'm not good enough for the Court of fire?"

"Court of Crimson," he corrected.

"Whatever." I waved my hands before propping them on my hips. "Do you think I'm not good enough?"

"It's not about being good enough," Roan said with

a grin. "It's just that Fae from the Court of Crimson are ... well, they're not like you."

The more my eyes narrowed, the wider his lips stretched. His smile irritated me—like he was laughing at my expense. "And what's that supposed to mean?" I grumbled irritably.

He chuckled, the sound low and vibrating. I felt like it reached deep within my body and lit a flame. My palms began to sweat. I wiped them down my sides. "No need to get defensive, little Changeling," he said. "I'm merely saying that you're not what I'd expect of a crimson Fae."

"What's a crimson Fae like then?" I asked.

Roan moved until he was pressed against me. Then he leaned down and a shiver stole through me as his lips brushed my ear as he spoke. "Crimson Fae are dangerous creatures. Full of blood and fire and sex," he whispered.

My thoughts poofed. They were there one second and gone the next. When Roan pulled away again, all I could do was blink up at him. Stunned. My jaw dropped as he gave me another smile, wicked and charming all at once. He nudged my face up.

"I'm here to find out why a creature such as yourself—like an innocent baby bird—would have an affinity for magic such as mine," he said.

Gods help me, but that sounded far more dangerous than nearly dying, and I wasn't at all sure I was ready to find out what he meant this time.

CHAPTER 18
CRESS

His words beat at my skin like my very pulse. *Full of blood and fire and sex. Blood and fire and sex. Fire and sex. Sex with Roan.* I had to bite my lip to stop the moan that was building within me from escaping. A shudder rippled through my body and I knew he felt it considering how he was pressed against me.

"Are you having naughty thoughts about me?" he asked, his voice a low growl next to me as his lips brushed against the delicate skin of the shell of my ear while his breath warmed my neck.

When a strangled sound of embarrassment escaped my throat, he chuckled. The dark sound sank into me and became one with my very bones. I knew in that moment as I stared up at eyes the color of glowing embers and hair I couldn't wait to run my fingers through that I wanted to hear that sound again. I'd do whatever I could to make that happen. Here in his room, alone with me, Roan was different. Gone was the cocky asshole, the brutish leader I'd first met; instead, there was a softer man, one who actually seemed to give a shit, and that was almost more than I could handle in my current state.

"What do you want, Roan?" I asked, my voice breathier than I would have liked.

"I told you, I want to find out why your body likes my magic so much," he replied with a grin.

"And we have to do this in your bedroom?"

"If we want privacy, yes. If you'd prefer the rest of the castle to watch then we can return to the throne room if you'd like?" He raised both his eyebrows in question, the dark red slashes mocking me, knowing that the last thing I would want was an audience.

"Here's fine," I said before sliding out from where he had pinned me to the wall.

Amusement danced in his eyes as he turned and watch me search for somewhere to sit that wasn't the bed. He had a writing desk that looked so fancy I was scared to touch it for fear that my very presence might destroy it somehow. Then there was an armchair that looked so overly stuffed that if I sat on it, it might explode. All of his room was done in dark tones of red, with bright areas coming from the sconces on the wall and the windows that opened up to the rays of daylight currently streaming through. It suddenly reminded me of a question I'd never had the chance to even ask let alone see if they would answer. They may not have before when they were suspicious of me being human but now that I was officially a Changeling

*—don't freak out, don't freak out, don't freak out—*I was hoping they'd be more honest with me, or at least give me a chance to process it before throwing the next test at me. That might be too much to ask of three Fae princes though.

"Why did you land the castle here? There's nothing around, it would take ages to get anywhere, and it's certainly not close to the battlefields. Why choose this valley?" I asked, crossing my arms over my chest as I stopped on the other side of his bed.

Roan's eyes tightened at the edges. Clearly, he hadn't expected my question and it made him tense. Why, I wasn't sure, but there was something behind it that bothered him, something he didn't want to tell me. "We just needed a break, little bird. It was either here or keep going to our final destination. As you said, this isn't near the battlefields, so we thought it would be a good place to stop."

He never looked away when he spoke to me and yet during that entire speech, he'd barely made eye contact with me. It was a lie. That much was as plain as the sun in the sky. Ever since he had almost scared me to death in the throne room, I had known that he'd been a very direct person, charismatic, but direct, in an almost off putting way; the way only a prince could be in my limited experience.

I wouldn't let that dissuade me though, so I asked, "Why did you just lie to me?"

His eyes shot to mine, a little wider than they had been a moment ago. "You accuse me of lying to you?"

He sounded astonished that someone would dare say such a thing. I was beginning to think that these princes had everyone in this castle licking their boots and thanking them for the opportunity to be helpful.

"I do. You just lied. I want to know why and I want to know what the truth is or I'll leave the room and won't let you test your precious Court of Crimson magic on me," I said.

I wasn't sure when I had become so brave with these men, but I was tired of being yanked around. I'd done what they asked, submitted to their tests, now all I wanted was some answers. That, surely, was not too much to ask.

"Fine, go, but if you do, you will be burning with your desire for me from the moment you set foot through those doors," he growled, heat washing into his gaze, and I knew he was pulling on his magic. He meant his threat literally. I thought of the warm heat that made me want to strip down in the library, that had me begging Orion for a glass of water, and had me tuning out everything anyone was saying because all I could focus on was the need to find some relief from it. That was not something I wanted to experience again, and yet I couldn't help but goad him slightly.

"Trying to get me to wander around the castle naked?" I teased. When he responded with a silent sneer I huffed out a sigh and finally sat down on the armchair, no longer caring if it exploded around me. Roan would deserve it if it did. It didn't though, and I sank into it as I imagined one would sink into a cloud. When I tried to readjust to find a better position that didn't have the cushions trying to swallow me whole I realized I couldn't move. I was stuck exactly where I was, the cushions of the chair holding me tightly in their fluffy grip. "Um, Roan? Why is your chair trying to eat me?"

A wicked smile curved the edge of his lips. "It's a safety precaution," he replied quietly as he rounded the bed and sat down opposite me.

"How is a chair a safety precaution?" I demanded.

"You can't get up, can you?" he asked, cocking an eyebrow at me.

I shook my head.

"So, if someone were to say, break into my room and wait for me so they could attack me, most likely they would take a seat, then when they try to get up... As a bonus, I get to see who wants to do me harm and interrogate them," he said, his voice turning cold at the end.

"People try to attack you?" I asked, suddenly wondering why he was even trusting me to be there if that was the case.

"Sorrell, Orion, and I are frequently at risk of assassination. I know Orion told you about the pixie taste testers. Well, we each have something in our rooms that keeps it secure from anyone it's not aligned to as well. It helps prevent some nasty surprises. Not all by any means, but some."

"So, this chair is rigged to trap anyone who sits in it

that's not you?" I asked to make sure I understood what he was saying.

He nodded and said, "Or Sorrell and Orion. The three of us never trap each other. It would leave us too vulnerable."

The seriousness with which he spoke sent a shiver down my spine. Their lives were constantly in danger. No wonder they'd reacted to me the way they had. Hell, that made Orion a little crazy if he was willing to go to bed with me and risk me trying to kill him. "Will you release me?" I asked, feeling vulnerable myself.

The wicked smile returned and made my insides melt and heat pool in my core. I'd just been with Orion and here I was lusting after Roan, but I didn't care. To me, it felt as natural as breathing, and I wasn't going to apologize for who I was, not anymore. That behavior could stay with the nuns and their shame ridden lives.

"Maybe. If you promise to let me experiment on you with my magic," he said finally, as he let his eyes roam over my body. I felt sexier in the shirt and pants than I had in the scraps of material they had called a dress the day before.

"Will you answer my question truthfully?" I asked.

Disappointment flashed across his features, and if I hadn't been staring at him I would have missed it. He'd been hoping that I had forgotten about his lie, about the question I'd asked, but I hadn't. I was more curious than a cat and it would probably get me killed one day but I was willing to risk it at least in that moment. "I will, if you'll answer one of mine truthfully," he countered.

"Deal," I replied, extending the one arm that wasn't suctioned to the armchair.

We shook like civilized beings. Tingles ran over my skin everywhere he touched me as we both grinned at each other as if we both knew it was a facade and neither of us was very good at being civilized. He was obviously more talented at faking it than I was, but there was a wildness hiding just underneath that I wanted to rile up and see explode out of this Fae until all the shreds of civility were gone. It didn't help that every time he smiled I could see it just a little more in the set of his jaw. Something about Roan drove me wild in a different way than Orion.

Roan muttered something and made a gesture with his hand and the armchair relaxed, the cushions deflating and turning to normal. I remained seated, I wasn't going to let some fabric and stuffing almost eating me scare me out of my comfy seat. I straightened my shirt and looked at Roan once more, staring him dead in the eye as I said, "So, why land the castle here?"

"It wasn't by choice," he said quietly, pausing for a moment as if to take in my reaction. When I didn't give one, simply sat there and blinked at him—waiting for the rest of it—he continued. "In each Fae Court, there is a Lanuaet. This is a magical device that we use to move the castles and Courts to ensure that we cannot be pinned down by the enemy. The device was designed to use the magic of four powerful Fae in combination to control the movements of the Court. We've found, over the years, that royals seem to be the only Fae capable of powering the Lanuaet. Unfortunately, however, as the years have progressed—with the war with humankind—bloodlines have grown thin. Where once there had been a multitude of royals to choose from, there are now very few."

"Four powerful Fae?" I repeated. "But there's only three of you."

He nodded. "Exactly. For our Court, we only have Orion, Sorrell, and me. Usually, we manage to handle it, but if we're not all in top form, completely charged with magic, then it becomes more challenging. We landed here because we had to. It was either land somewhere we knew was safe or risk landing in a dangerous zone or on top of a human settlement when we ran out of power." He pulled a hand through the dark red locks of his hair and I watched as I processed the words he'd just said.

"And, just for clarification purposes, you charge your magic with sex?"

He nodded, a wicked grin curving his lips. "Want to try?"

I ignored his suggestion and said, "So, it had nothing to do with the area or with me? It was just because one of you didn't get laid enough?" I asked, a small smile curving my lips in return even though I didn't mean for it to happen.

He shook his head with a chuckle. "Sorry to disappoint, little bird, but we didn't know you were here," he replied.

Somehow, I thought the three of them were drowning in willing partners, but whether they actually took them to bed or not I couldn't say, and I tried not to care either. I wanted to know more, so much more, about how this castle worked and what it meant to be a Changeling that the feeling was almost overwhelming. Everything in my life had changed so quickly and so completely that I felt like a totally different person than the girl who had stumbled into the castle in her nightdress.

"I wonder if that had anything to do with the noise I heard," I mused aloud, intending for the words to only be for myself.

Roan's eyes sought my gaze. "What noise?"

"The night I stumbled into the castle, well, earlier that day, I'd woken up to this awful screeching noise that was so bad my ears were bleeding and the nuns had to sedate me to get me to stop screaming. Once the sedation wore off it was night and the castle was here. It's why I was just in a nightdress when I was wandering around," I replied, feeling unsure about sharing something so private with him.

"The Lanuaet was fighting us that day, resisting the directions we were giving it, which is why it was taking so much magic to make it move the castle."

"And it wasn't working?" I asked.

"No, it was working, but it was fighting us, like it had a mind of its own or something. It's always loud to us when we use it, but I've never heard of it being loud to someone else, and to hear it across a distance like that... I'll have to get Sorrell to do some research on it, or maybe even Groffet. That dwarf is a wizard at finding out obscure pieces of information, not literally though. I just wish I knew why it was fighting us." His voice had gone distant as though he was remembering how it had felt to work with the magic while it was fighting him, and I could see lines of strain pop up on his face.

"Has it ever done that before?" I asked, hopefully breaking the replay of the memory, I knew from experience that those could be painful to be stuck in.

He shook his head. We both sat in silence mulling over the information we had shared. After a moment Roan looked up at me, his eyes sparkling once again and he said, "Want to see what kind of Crimson magic you've got?"

I nodded, at least that would be something that could be useful in the future. I might have real, live magic and not know it, and if Roan could help me find it then I was all for it, even if he was a dick sometimes.

CHAPTER 19
ROAN

She was a curious little thing, Cress. Unique in a way that I'd never seen before. Then again, I shouldn't have been surprised since she was the first Changeling I'd ever met. Changelings in lore were known to be powerful and I assumed she would be, but Changelings were also often ostracized for their upbringing. With how things were between mankind and Fae, it wouldn't surprise me if she would be as well. So far, she'd only had to deal with me, Orion, and Sorrell, but soon the time would come that she'd have to be released on the rest of the Court.

My thoughts permeated my actions as I led her to an open section of the room. A place where the stone floor had been charred and left black by many a spell I'd cast there. She let me lead her and position her as I would without a fight, and as I circled her, stepping close to her back, I leaned down and inhaled her unique scent.

"Lift your arms," I commanded gruffly. She did as I ordered, her arms rising up, pale and slender as I watched. In this, I was the composer and she was my instrument. "Repeat after me." I waited for her to nod before I recited an old incantation—one of the first I'd learned in my lessons of magic—as I touched her and pushed some of my magic into her skin. She repeated my words in a soft whisper and within moments, a glow began to form along her flesh. I moved away from her back and returned to her front once more, noting how her eyes had widened as she stared at her hands and arms—glowing and getting brighter as time went on.

"What did I do?" she asked.

"It's a light spell," I answered. "Nothing too dangerous."

She waved her arms up and down, flapping them like a bird might flap its wings and I found myself chuckling at the movement. "No, stop that." I reached forward and caught her hands in mine. She froze, her small face tipped back as she stared up at me. I felt the magic leave her skin and sink into me. Her arms and hands lost their glow.

"What else can I do?" She whispered the question.

I blinked, realizing how close I'd gotten to her. So close that we were nearly chest to chest. I could feel her breath on me. I released her and backed up. "We don't know yet, but we do know that you have a capacity for magic, so you're definitely a Changeling."

"Does that mean no more tests?" she asked, louder than before.

I nodded. "I don't see why it'd be necessary."

She tilted her head to the side, white-blonde hair sliding over her shoulders. "What's the Court of Crimson like?" she asked suddenly.

An automatic stiffness stole over my shoulders, atrophying my muscles. The feeling spread, moving into my chest and down my arms and legs making it difficult for me to turn away and stride back across the room. "It's a Fae Court like any other," I said without looking up.

"Then why won't you look at me when you say that?" she asked, the sound of her footsteps following me as I moved to a table with a pitcher on it. I stopped at the table and retrieved a glass, pouring some of the fresh water into it before lifting the cup to my lips and downing it. "Roan?"

I shook my head. It didn't matter how many times I reminded her, she continued with that damn name. No prince or my Lord for her. No, she went straight for the name. "The Court of Crimson is a dangerous Court," I finally admitted, keeping my gaze on the surface of the table, tracing the marks and scars that had been left from many years of use.

"Why?" she pressed, curiosity coloring her tone.

Memories surfaced—of blood sacrifices, of cold faces, of Franchesca's betrayal. My hand clamped around the glass in my fist until it shattered. I turned abruptly and glared at the source of my irritation.

"It just is," I gritted out. "Leave it alone."

With that, I shook out my hand, letting the glass shards rain down on the tabletop. "Call the pixies to clean this up," I ordered before turning and striding from the room.

CHAPTER 20
CRESS

Roan left the room angry. I didn't understand it, but even after I called the pixies to help clean up the broken cup he'd left behind, I couldn't find the patience to wait for him to come back. I left Roan's bedroom and began searching the castle. Instead of finding him, however, I found myself back in the library where I'd passed out from magic overload. As I strode into the room, curving around a stack of books taller than myself, I heard a grumble followed by a grunt and then watched as a landslide of books fell off of a nearby table onto a small creature.

"Hello?" I called out as several books were swatted away and the small creature squirmed and wiggled out of the pile all the while cursing quietly.

The whispers cut off. "Yes?" the creature called back.

"Do you need some help?"

"I wouldn't be averse to it," the creature replied.

The prim way he said it made me grin as I got on my knees and began lifting books away from his small body until I uncovered a rather hairy little man with a long scraggly gray beard and a crooked nose. I blinked at him and he blinked back.

"What are you?" I blurted.

"I am not a what," he huffed, getting to his feet and dusting himself off. "I am a who. I'm Groffet, my lady." He held out his hand. "Prince Sorrell's personal steward, at your service."

"Steward?" I took his hand anyway even as I frowned in confusion.

"Yes. You must be the Changeling."

"That's me—how'd you know?"

"Young lady,"—Groffet found a pair of spectacles on the ground and lifted them up, holding them in front of his face and grimacing at the single crack that ran down the center of one lens—"I have been around for quite some time and I have been Master Sorrell's steward for the last twenty years or so. You are not the first Changeling I've ever met. There's a tell."

"There is?" My eyes widened and I nearly choked as I watched Groffet point one fat, grubby finger at the crack of his lens and run the tip of his finger down the fissure, and as he did so, the broken pieces sealed themselves together, leaving behind nothing but a perfect pair of spectacles. "How did you do that?" I demanded.

Groffet placed his glasses on his nose, pushing them up until they settled against his face perfectly before he looked at me. "Magic," he answered. "And there is—your wonderment is tell enough."

I scooted back as the small man got up and waddled around me, waving his finger again. My mouth popped open as books began to ascend from where they'd fallen and restack themselves on the nearest surface. Some remained on the floor, some lifted and settled on the table and some flew about the room until they found places on the shelves and squeezed themselves in.

"Mother of the Gods..." I breathed in startled bewilderment, "that's amazing."

"It's nothing," Groffet commented as he moved towards the platform in the center of the room and continued up the staircase in the back until he reached the desk. "Now," he clambered up into the seat, pressed a lever and was lifted until the top of his hat was visible over the top, "what can I do for you, young Changeling?"

"Um..." I glanced around. "You can tell me where the guys are?"

"Guys?" he repeated, lifting up further in his seat until he stood and leaned over the top of the desk. "You wouldn't, perhaps, be referring to the princes, would you?"

I nodded. "Yeah, them."

"*Guys*," he muttered, shaking his head. Had I said something wrong? "Prince Sorrell is reading in his personal study; I would highly recommend not interrupting him, and Prince Orion is—"

"What about Roan?" I interrupted.

"Prince Roan is unavailable," Groffet said.

I frowned. "Why?"

Groffet lifted one bushy eyebrow. "Why is he unavailable?"

"Yes," I said. "Why is he unavailable? Where is he? What is he doing? He was supposed to teach me Crimson magic." Groffet chuckled lowly. "Is that funny?" I asked.

Instead of answering, he clambered back down from his chair and continued to chuckle as he descended the stairs and began waddling around the room, flicking his finger in the air—pointing to various shelves as books came flying out. I ducked when one almost collided with my head. Another sailed over my shoulder, nearly clipping me in the side. I backed away from the flying books as Groffet collected another mountainous stack of them at his side.

Finally, when it appeared that he was done, he turned to me and gestured me forward. Slowly—hesitantly—I stepped away from my safe place against the wall and moved towards him. "Take these," he said, nodding to the stack of books. "Read them. Study them and you just might be able to learn something."

"What are they?" I asked.

Groffet's spectacles gleamed in the light as he tipped his head back and looked at me through the lenses perched on the end of his bulbous nose. "They're the complete history of Fae Courts. Start at the top, you'll learn everything you need to about

Prince Roan's Court of Crimson before you start anything else."

I stopped beside the stack and lifted the first book, reading the title: "The Complete Works of Magnus Crimson." I arched a brow at Groffet. "Who's Magnus Crimson?"

Groffet shook his head and flipped his finger at me. A force unlike any other overcame me and my whole body was spun back towards the library's doors. My feet lifted and marched me—against my will—not stopping until I landed in the corridor outside the library.

"Magnus Crimson was the first King of Crimson," Groffet said.

I turned around, wiggling my fingers and toes and frowning down at my body as I made sure I had full control once more. "Why do I—"

Groffet shook his head as he appeared on the other side of the library's entryway, both hands latched on the doors. "Read the book, child," he ordered. "Then direct your questions to Prince Roan, himself."

"But—"

The doors slammed shut, echoing throughout the empty hallway and leaving me even more baffled than before. I simply stood there for a moment, staring at the closed doors of the library before I glanced back down at the book in my hand. *Well, it was a starting point,* I supposed. I turned and headed off again. *A starting point was better than nothing.*

CHAPTER 21
CRESS

I hadn't planned on falling asleep in the throne room, it just kind of happened. The books that Groffet gave me weren't exactly exciting reading material. Falling asleep wasn't quite the shock, but waking up left me groggy. Something had woken me, but I wasn't sure what. I pulled myself together, straightening my clothes, and wiping the drool away from my mouth and the book I'd fallen asleep on. I hoped Groffet didn't mind too much. I cringed at the dried saliva that was still stuck to the page. Hopefully, he wouldn't notice.

My hands were midway through finger combing my hair when I heard Ariana's laugh. It was distinctive in a way that only a laugh that belongs to someone you loathe could be. The hair on the nape of my neck stood on end and my teeth clenched so hard that the back of my jaw twinged slightly. I took a deep breath in through my nose and slowly let it out through my mouth as I tried to center myself before she and her cronies arrived. Maybe they wouldn't see me. I was tucked back in the corner, after all. I hadn't intended on hiding—I'd just found a comfortable space to read the book Groffet had given me—but now it worked in my favor.

I ducked my head and opened the book once more, turning to the last page I remembered before I'd fallen asleep. I'd keep reading about Magnus Crimson, and hope that at some point, I would get to where he stopped regaling the reader with his sexual conquests and started talking about actual magic. So far, all I'd learned was that the Crimson Court, founded in his name, was one of the most sexually active and adventurous Courts and all of it was because of him. I wondered how many children he must have had. Other than some explicit sexual conquests on ladies from various Courts, the only thing of true value I'd learned so far was that there used to be a whole lot more Fae Courts than there were currently. I mean, hundreds of Fae Courts—all spaced out across the land—and yet, from the small footnotes at the bottom of various pages, I learned that there were maybe a couple dozen left. *What had caused that?* I wondered.

"Ugh. I don't want to eat in here if *it's* in here," Ariana's voice sounded, echoing all around the room. There was no doubt that she wanted me to hear. I didn't react, though, didn't allow myself a flinch or even a blink as I continued scanning the page in front of me. "Ladies, let's get a plate and leave. Apparently, it's not even smart enough to know when it's being spoken to."

This time, I did raise my eyes, and I shot her a glare that I hoped was pure fire, something to burn her from the inside out. My glares must have been defective or something, though, because it had no effect. Go figure, I'd be just the girl to try and glare her way out of a problem and instead of looking deadly or dangerous, I probably looked like my eyes were broken. Could someone even glare their way out of trouble? I'd have to try it next time—not that I was thinking there definitely *would* be a next time, but for research purposes, if there *was*, in fact, a next time, I'd try it out.

Ariana, bitch of all bitches, approached me and pulled me from my thoughts. I met her gaze with one of my glares—*come on glare powers*, I thought. *Intensify or something.* Her silvery eyes remained cool and distant. "So, you do understand me."

"Of course, I understand you," I replied, even though I knew I shouldn't engage her in conversation, especially when it seemed the power of my glare wasn't doing anything.

"Lady Ariana. That's what you should say. 'Of course, I understand you, Lady Ariana.' I am a Lady of the Courts, most likely to be Roan's next fiancée. You will address me with respect or I will have you thrown in the dungeon."

They had a dungeon? Honestly, I wouldn't be surprised if she wasn't bluffing. This was a castle after all. *Didn't all castles come with dungeons?* And if anyone was going to throw me in one, it would be Ariana.

"Yes, *Lady Ariana*," I replied, trying to sound as snooty as she had as I spoke. Even as I did, my brain finally caught up to what she'd said. Next fiancée? Roan? That couldn't be accurate. Roan didn't seem to particularly care for Ariana—okay, he might have felt her up a bit when I'd first come around but did that mean he really liked her?—and if he didn't, why would she think he'd want to marry her? Maybe it was just a political thing? He was a prince after all. Whatever the case was, I didn't like it. It made my chest feel tight and my stomach twist into knots. Then again, that could've been because I hadn't eaten since I woke up.

"Leave," Ariana snapped. "My ladies and I wish to eat in peace, not being hovered over by some mongrel half-breed."

I rolled my eyes. A part of me wanted to fight her, to tell her to go to the deepest circle of hell, but the truth was, I just didn't have the energy for dealing with her. Not when I was trying to figure my own stuff out. She wasn't worth it.

Though it was a struggle, I gathered the books Groffet had given me and left, wandering out of the throne room as Ariana and her company of girls laughed at my back and started up with the insults once more. If there was a spell in Groffet's books that would sew their fucking mouths shut, I intended to find it. I meandered through the castle until I found myself outside of Roan's room once more. Hefting the books against my chest, I reached up and knocked as hard as I could while holding the pile. When no answer greeted me, I debated what to do next. I could go and find Roan or I could try and find Orion, since his room was the only other place I knew of in this section of the castle.

At the thought of walking back through the corridors and trying to find my way to his room, though, the books in my grip suddenly felt like they gained weight. I didn't want to amble around with these books anymore. I was tired, cranky, kinda hungry, and these books were freaking heavy. I knocked on the door again, more firmly this time.

After a moment, the telltale sounds of footsteps approached from the other side, the knob turned, and the door creaked open to reveal a half naked Roan with a towel wrapped around his waist and water droplets clinging to his skin. My eyes widened as I watched as whatever magical heat emitting from his body made the droplets evaporate from his skin and turn to steam. I swallowed against a dry throat. Holy Gods, he was ... divination in Fae form. He had to be a demi god or something because I'd never seen a man who looked like *that*. His muscles could've been carved from stone. Orion, I'd thought, was ripped, but Roan was chiseled. Pure fucking ropes of muscle and sinew and skin—and was I drooling? I reached up and wiped at the corner of my mouth as I juggled the books. Yup. There was a little bit of drool. Had he noticed?

As soon as his eyes settled on mine, Roan nodded

and turned from the door, allowing me to come in and nudge it shut with my foot before looking for somewhere to set the pile in my arms down.

"I see Groffet loaded you up on history books, hmmm?" Roan asked.

"He did?" I couldn't stop staring. When he glanced back at me with a frown, I straightened abruptly. "I mean, he did. Yes. Books—history. I read them sometimes. I can read." I jerked my gaze down to the pile still in my arms and then back up to see him turn back to his wardrobe.

He chuckled as he dropped the towel and by Coreliath's fucking beard, I thought I might perish. Right there and then. In fact, I was a little shocked I hadn't already gone up in smoke. His butt—mother of Gods—I was drooling again. I really needed to stop that. I lifted my books back up my chest as I struggled to wipe the drool from my chin. "H-he told me to start there instead of with you. I was reading them in the throne room since I don't have a place to stay, but Ariana found me in there and kicked me out so I just … I didn't know where else to go," I ended lamely.

"Out of the frying pan, into the fire," Roan said, pulling on a pair of loose trousers. When he turned to face me it was like the world slowed down for just a moment as my eyes greedily devoured every inch of exposed skin, every curve of muscle. He hadn't even done up the laces. All the water was gone and his hair was dry. I tried to picture him strutting around the castle in just a towel and couldn't, at least not without causing the females to faint at just the sight of him.

By the Gods, it should've been impossible to be so attractive.

I must have loosened my grip on the books because the next thing I knew they were falling from my grasp onto the floor and my toes. I cursed before dropping to the floor to pick them up. Surprisingly, Roan's hands were there a moment later.

"Groffet will be most unhappy if you damage one of his books," the Fae prince cautioned.

I looked up at him, at the fire dancing in the depths of his eyes, at the flame red hair that I wanted to run my hands through, at the lush lips I wanted to bite and suck and slide my tongue over. Roan was temperamental, just like fire itself. He needed to be encouraged, fed the right thoughts to see him flourish, but he could turn on you in a snap if you betrayed him. I could sense it from the way he was hesitant with me, the way he was different when we were alone versus when we were with the others.

"Are you engaged to Ariana?" The question blurted from my mouth before I could stop it. The fire I'd seen glowing in his eyes seemed to stutter out and they turned cold and dark.

"No, why would you think that?" His voice was a low, vicious growl.

"She was bragging about possibly getting engaged to you when she kicked me out of the throne room—

she said she was going to be your next fiancée," I replied, noting his flinch at the word *next*.

"Yes, she's been hinting at it for a while now," he said with a low, irritated snarl.

"You don't seem all that happy about it," I commented.

Roan was quiet for a moment, his head lowering as he continued to gather books in his arms. "She's not the only one who has been hinting at it," he admitted.

"Who else?" I asked.

He froze. Then, in a nearly indiscernible whisper, he hissed. "My mother wants the union as well." He lifted his head, his gaze meeting mine. Roan's eyes darkened and the fire I'd seen there earlier was back. This time, however, it was a raging inferno of powerlessness.

I may not have ever had a parent, but I had the nuns, and I knew what being powerless against those who held sway over your life felt like. I'd been ridiculed, called lazy, a burden, and difficult among other things. I hadn't been able to stomach meat or a lot of the food the nuns had served and since coming to the Fae Court, that hadn't been a problem. Their food didn't taste like rocks on my tongue or churn in my gut and make my stomach coil and knot up. There, I hadn't possessed any agency over my own life. Here—I was still somewhat out of my depth, but I didn't feel completely powerless.

Even if I couldn't be in charge of myself yet, one day I hoped to be free to do whatever the hell I wanted.

When that happened, I'd finally be able to do all of the things I'd wanted to. I'd travel, visit new and interesting places, meet people, and just live to be free. But big changes didn't happen overnight. It was one day at a time, one small step after another. All I knew now was that I was on my path towards freedom, inching ever closer, and no one was going to stop me.

Roan handed over the books he'd picked up and stood, taking a step away from me. We locked eyes, but neither of us said a word. Instead, silence descended over the room. I sat, surrounded by books on the floor, while Roan paced around the room, burning off his anger. I blinked when a few times, his hands went up in flames only to disperse a second later, his skin perfectly fine. When his pacing slowed and he hadn't set anything ablaze for a while I tempted fate by asking, "What did she mean when she said she'd be your *next* fiancée?"

Roan was pacing away from me when I spoke but when the question left my lips, he stopped. He didn't look back but remained right where he was. He didn't move, didn't even look like he was breathing for so long that I was beginning to worry. I adjusted the books on my lap and stacked them to the side as I got up off the floor. Not a twitch, not even a blink—nothing that I could see that would give me any indication that he had heard me and hadn't just frozen on the spot.

As I debated what to do, Roan finally looked back over his shoulder. His face was etched in agony. "Her name was Franchesca," he said, his voice barely above a whisper. "We met when we were children."

I took a step towards him and he turned, facing me completely. "Roan?"

He shook his head and continued. "We grew up together in my mother's Court. The Court of Crimson."

"Was she a Crimson Fae too?" I asked.

He nodded. "But she wasn't..." He stopped, swallowing as he closed his eyes and reached up with both hands to scrub his palms against his face. When his arms dropped back down to his sides, he reopened his eyes. "Chesca was my best friend," he said, and as he stared at me, his eyes shone with some sort of fiery light, and I felt like he was trying to tell me something. As if he were begging me not to judge him for the emotion currently covering his face.

I strode towards him, not stopping until I was right in front of him. "It's okay," I said, reaching out and taking one of his hands.

His eyes never left my face. "She wasn't royal," he said as if imparting some secret. "Her family was lower in the Court. They had migrated from an older Court that no longer had a royal line. We were young when I asked her to marry me. My mother didn't approve. She was my world, though. My father is gone now, but even before he died, my parents didn't have the type of union I'd always wanted for myself."

"What kind of union?" I asked.

He inhaled, his eyelids lowering once more as he

breathed out through his mouth. "Crimson Fae are sexual," he said.

"Really?" I chuckled lightly. "You could've fooled me."

His eyes opened and he shot me a look. I shrugged, but he shook his head. By the curl at the corner of his mouth, I'd accomplished what I'd set out to do. Break some of the tension. His hand squeezed mine. "My parents' union was cold. They came together to procreate, but not much else. Of my five brothers and sisters, I am the only surviving heir."

I gaped. "They're all dead?"

Roan tilted his head to the side. "This war with the humans has taken many lives," was all he said in response to that question. I didn't know what else to say to that, so I simply nodded and he continued. "Chesca and I were engaged for several months, at which point I was being groomed to take the throne. Several weeks before what would have been our wedding, she came to me and offered herself. We'd already come together so many times, but love is strange—I trusted her completely. I thought she was my life mate. After we had joined and I'd fallen asleep, though, I woke to find her lifting a dagger over my chest. Had I not woken when I did, she would have killed me. As it turns out, her family had been plotting to overthrow the Court of Crimson for some time. Without an heir, the Court of Crimson would have fallen."

My breath caught in my chest as his voice grew

tighter with each spoken word. He sounded hollow, as though he was talking about someone else's past and not his own. It reminded me somewhat of how Nellie had spoken when she talked about losing her parents. I couldn't even imagine trusting someone so much and wanting to spend my life with them only to be betrayed by them.

"I'm so sorry, Roan," I whispered, my voice quiet as I reached for his other hand. I looked up into his face, keeping his eyes with mine. "No one should have to go through something like that."

"If I was a stronger man I would have asked her why," he said. "I still wonder if any of it was real or if she thinks about me, if she regrets it."

I frowned. "She's still alive?"

"In the dungeon of my mother's Court," he said with a nod. "Surrounded and imprisoned by iron—completely devoid of her magic. It's the absolute worst punishment for a Fae other than death." He pulled his hands from mine and took a step back, moving to the bed.

I tried to keep myself from going to him, but I couldn't, not when the pain that was radiating out of him was so brutal and sharp. He'd given his heart to this woman and she'd tried to murder him. My feet carried me towards the bed, and as I approached, I reached for him, unable to stop myself from doing anything else.

As soon as my skin connected with his, it felt like a match had been struck. All the air seemed to be sucked out of the room as I crawled onto the bed and reached around, awkwardly hugging his back to my chest. I felt it when he inhaled sharply, his chest shooting up and holding when he didn't release the breath right away.

I don't know what told me to say what I did, but without thinking, I let the words spill from me. "I'm not her," I said. "I'm me. I do my own thing, react my own way, screw things up, react badly to Fae Court politics that are normal for you. I want to learn about magic and Court life and customs, but I don't want you to think I'm her, trying to weasel my way in for some ulterior motive. Before I even came here, I had one friend in the whole world. She'd probably hate me now if she knew what I was. The only people I have now are you, Orion, and Sorrell—well, if Sorrell can stop being such a butthead to me, but you get my meaning."

Roan burst out laughing and pulled from my arms before turning to face me. "Ahhh, Cress. Sorrell is the best of us all. He's as loyal as they come. He saved me from myself and my grief and anger after Chesca. He saved Orion when he was fighting on the frontlines. We each have our stories to tell, but I assure you, Ariana is not going to be my next fiancée—even if my mother approves of it. I'll have to correct her. This has been enlightening, little bird. Thank you."

He moved to stand from the bed, but before he could, I took the opportunity to ask, "Can I read in here since I don't have anywhere else?"

"For now. I'll get the pixies to make you up a room,

clothes and all, then you'll have your own space, but for now, I need to go and have a chat with Ariana."

It wasn't until after Roan had left and I was halfway down another page of sexual exploits in the book about Magnus Crimson that I realized my mistake. Roan was going to talk with Ariana and there was no doubt—she'd know it was me that turned her in. *What if she retaliated even further?*

After a moment of contemplation, I cursed and put the book down. I needed to find out exactly what Roan was going to say to her, perhaps stop him if it was too horrible. I hurried from the room, hoping I wasn't too late.

CHAPTER 22
ROAN

Ariana was still in the throne room when I arrived. She cackled with several other women at one of the high tables, but I knew when she sensed my approach. Her head lifted and a seductive grin curled her lips. I frowned as I stomped down the aisles of banquet tables while the pixies flitted back and forth cleaning up messes and bringing in more food.

"Darling," she called, standing from her seat as I stopped before her.

"We need to talk," I said.

She smiled brightly. "Goodness," she said, putting a hand to her chest, "I didn't believe you'd want to do this here."

My brows pinched together as my frown deepened until I realized what she meant. I shook my head. "Ariana, I have neither the intention nor the desire to ask you to be my fiancée," I said.

Her smile fell away as her mouth gaped open.

Every single Fae in the vicinity went silent. Eyes were rooted on the two of us, but she had brought this upon herself. I was not a cruel man, but neither was I a patient one, and I was quite finished with her assumptions and petty manipulation. I moved closer, dropping my voice. "You warmed my bed," I said. "That was all. We were playmates, nothing more."

"Were?" It seemed she was in shock. She lifted her chin and stared at me, confusion etched into her features as she began to shake her head back and forth. "I don't understand what you're saying." Her palm lifted. She reached for me. I took a step back.

"Yes," I stated flatly. "Whatever we were is no longer possible. I cannot and will not lay with you if you believe that you have a chance at marriage."

Ariana breathed in and out through her nose so sharply that she resembled an angry bull. When her eyes lifted and zeroed in over my shoulder, I turned my head back. "*You*." The vehemence that spat from Ariana's lips was only a precursor to her wrath.

No sooner had I seen Cress stop just inside the room and Ariana was circling me and heading straight for her. "You did this!" she shrieked. "You turned him against me!"

Before I could predict what she might do, Ariana released a bolt of fire magic from her fingertips. I watched in horror as the flames arched out and slammed into the Changeling's chest, sending her flying out of the room and into the corridor. Her back slammed into the stone wall with an audible noise.

"Enough!" My voice boomed across the room, making tables and plates alike tremble. Ariana whipped around as if just realizing her error. My anger snapped through me and I felt flames dance against the nape of my neck as I descended the high table and headed for her.

"My Lord," she said quickly, "I'm so sorry, I didn't realize what I was doing. I—"

Her words were cut off when my hand closed around her throat. "You disrespect me," I growled lowly.

"No!" She shook her head back and forth, eyes widening in true fear. "I swear, I—"

"*Silence!*"

She clamped her mouth shut, trembling in my grip. Two figures appeared in the doorway to the throne room. Orion and Sorrell. Orion went to the Changeling while Sorrell approached me.

"Roan." His voice was quiet, reserved. Gentle even. I did not want to be gentle. I wanted to unleash my anger. It was held barely in check, just beneath the surface of my flesh, writhing with the desire to be let out. "Release her."

"No." My voice was flat. I didn't even look at Orion as he lifted the Changeling into his arms. She was unconscious, that much I knew. "Take her to my chambers, Orion," I bit out. In my periphery, I noticed that my words gave him pause. He glanced to Sorrell and only when Sorrell nodded did he continue off down the hallway. That, too, angered me. How dare he not follow my orders immediately! In my irritation, I didn't realize that my grasp on Ariana's throat had tightened.

Sorrell put a hand on my arm. "You're strangling her, Roan."

"Good," I snapped. "This is what happens when an unranked Fae attempts to manipulate a royal, when an unranked Fae disrespects a royal."

"Roan, release her to me," Sorrell tried again. "I will ensure that she spends some time in the iron dungeons, reflecting on her actions."

I shivered with the need to contract my grip even harder. I watched Ariana's squirms as, for the first time ever, she was completely meek and submissive. Her eyes pleaded with me even as she struggled to breathe. Before I could change my mind, I released her throat.

"To your chambers," I ordered.

"Yes, my Lord," she croaked, getting up and practically running from the room.

When no one else spoke or made a move to leave, I turned to the rest of them. "All of you," I ordered. "Get out. This space is off limits for the foreseeable future. You may take your meals in your chambers or anywhere else. For now, get the fuck out of my throne room."

There was a flurry of activity as the rest of the Fae moved to follow my orders. Several ran from the room, many followed at a much slower pace—watching as Sorrell guided me to the side. The pixies had disappeared almost as soon as magic had been unleashed. I felt heat building beneath my skin. When still there remained a few slower Fae, I grew impatient. "*Get out!*" I roared, sending them scrambling as they bolted to the exit. As soon as the last Fae was gone, I waved a hand and the doors to the throne room slammed shut. I turned and a pixie flitted down from the ceiling. I curled a finger at the creature and it hesitantly followed my silent command. "Get rid of the food," I snapped. "I want the tables gone. Everything." It nodded its little head and then pixies poured from the ceiling and walls—rushing to do as I'd ordered.

"Roan, what is this about?" Sorrell asked, calling my attention back to him.

"This is about me reminding our subjects who is royal here and who is not," I growled.

Sorrell sighed. "It's not just about that," he said. "It's the Changeling, isn't it?" He shook his head and turned away. "She's not staying, Roan. Don't get attached."

"Since when did we decide that?" I snapped. It took me two steps to reach him. I grabbed his shoulder and pulled him around to meet my gaze. "The Changeling's fate hasn't yet been decided."

Sorrell gaped at me. "We don't even know for sure if she is a Changeling!"

"She handled the magic test *you* wanted to put her through."

"She passed out," he replied.

"But she didn't die," I said. "She would have if she were human. Her survival proves that she's a Changeling!"

"What is this really about?" Sorrell demanded, pulling back from me as he cut me a glare with those cold eyes of his like fucking shards of ice.

"Ariana is out of control," I stated. "She was laboring under the impression that I was going to make her my next fiancée and as you well fucking know that won't be happening."

Sorrell grimaced. "Your mother expects you to choose someone, Roan."

"I know," I replied through gritted teeth even as I shoved a hand through my hair, pausing just long enough to grab a hunk of the stuff and yank at it in frustration. "But not her. I will not marry her."

"Okay." Sorrell's voice lost its edge as he moved slowly towards me again. "It's okay, Roan. You don't have to decide now."

"She'll expect it at some point, but I don't—I can't—it's not the right time. We're in the middle of a war."

"I know." A knock sounded on the door, loud and disruptive. There were only a few people left in this castle that would knock like that after the scene that had just been observed by half of the Court.

Sorrell backed away and I dropped my hand as he called for the person on the other side to come in. The door opened and Groffet waddled into the throne room, eyeing me. "My Lords," he said, nodding in respectful acknowledgment.

"Did you check on the girl?" I asked.

He nodded. "She is still asleep, but I have given her an elixir that should have her injuries healed soon."

"How bad were they?"

"Her injuries?" he inquired, tilting his head.

"No, her fucking breasts—yes, her injuries," I snapped.

Groffet blinked. "Her injuries from the magic are minor, sir. She merely hit her head against the stone. Her breasts are average."

I slapped a palm over my face. The old bastard knew I couldn't kill him. He was far too valuable. "Thank you, Groffet," Sorrell said before I could say or do anything else. "You may go."

Groffet nodded, turning around and waddling back towards the throne room doors. As soon as the old man was out of the room, I flipped back to Sorrell. "I'm going to her," I said.

"Are you sure that's a good idea?" he asked, grabbing my arm as I took a step towards the doors. "In your condition, you could hurt her. And you do seem rather concerned with the girl's well being."

I paused and arched a brow at him. "What condition is that?"

"You're riled, Roan, and we both know what happens when you're like that. Look at your hair." I hadn't even noticed, but he was right. Flames danced through the strands of my hair, circling my head in a halo of fire. He released me as I reached up and patted them out, sucking in a deep breath and letting it out as I forced the tension in my shoulders to ease.

"I'll be fine," I said after a moment.

"Roan!" Sorrell called after me as I stomped away.

"Later," I called back.

Right now, I needed to ensure that the Changeling was alright. Even Fae could be hurt by fire magic. I couldn't explain it, but there was a strange desire taking root inside of me to make sure that the girl—Cress—was okay, and this time, I wouldn't deny it.

CHAPTER 23
CRESS

I woke up feeling like I was burning in hellfire. Sweat rolled down my temples and around to my neck where my head rested on a pillow. Gods, it was hot. Hotter than hot. Was I boiling alive? It felt like it. I cracked my eyes open but the room was so dark I couldn't see anything. All I knew was that I had two heavy bands across me, one that went from my shoulders and curved over my breasts, tucking behind my waist, and another that I soon realized wasn't a band at all but a leg that was thrown across my right leg, the knee of the person's leg dangerously close to areas only Orion had touched.

My hands tentatively reached up awkwardly and confirmed that the band around my chest was, in fact, an arm. It didn't feel like Orion's though. No scars. So, who was holding me? I tried to ease away from the mystery person but didn't get very far before they tightened their grip and pulled me even closer than before. Close enough to feel everything about their body, and how naked they were, which made me realize how naked *I* was, which was when I started to get concerned.

If it wasn't Orion who the hell was touching me? Roan? It didn't seem likely since he had told me himself he didn't literally sleep with others after everything with Franchesca, so why would he with me now? It made no sense. I nudged whoever was cuddling me into an early grave and hoped I could wake them before I lost all the fluid in my body. I tried to track back in my mind, to remember how I got wherever I was, but the last thing I remembered was a furious Ariana and fire.

I nudged the person next to me harder until I heard a grumpy mumble from somewhere around my shoulder. Finally, I gave up trying to be gentle and rolled towards them, pushing them. "Hey," I hissed as loud as I dared. "Wake up."

Three things happened all at once. The lights in the room turned on, blinding me, I was rolled onto my back and pinned down, and not in a particularly sexy way. Finally, when I could see again I realized I was being pinned down by someone that, in that moment, looked more like an avenging angel than a Fae. A ring of fire circled Roan's head. It resembled a crown and lit up the area around us, illuminating his face. Flames licked down his hair to his shoulders as his normally red hair bled to white. His amber eyes seemed to glow as bright as embers of a fire as they looked through me.

To top that off, his skin was practically luminescent. He looked like he could set this whole place on fire if he wanted to with just a thought.

Given the vicious snarl on his face and the way he was baring his teeth at me I knew he wasn't in his right mind. Whatever was happening right now, he was reliving his memories with Franchesca and not seeing me. One of the hands that was pinning my wrists down came around to my throat, resting on it and slowly squeezing as he snarled at me. I got the feeling he thought he was saying words but I couldn't understand them in his current state.

"Roan," I said softly. "I'm not her. I'm Cress, the Changeling. Cressida. Please, you're starting to hurt me." As I spoke his grip tightened. My free hand came up and began clawing at his hand that was around my throat. I realized that was pointless, he was stronger than me and had magic; he could kill me in a second if he wanted to. I took a deep calming breath—well, as much as I could with his hand around my throat, and instead lifted my hand up even further to cup his face. "Roan, look at me." He flinched but his gaze was still distant. "Hey, remember when you accused me of breaking into the castle, then demanded I have sex with you to get the human smell off me? Or when you threw magic at me to see if I was a Changeling? Then decided I was part of the Court of Crimson? Remember all that? That happened with me, with Cress, not with her."

As I spoke I saw the recognition flicker back to his

eyes, but when he made contact with mine, panic filled his as he took in the scene around him. Instead of calming down like I'd hoped it made him even worse. The flames in his hair that had been orange and yellow in color turned a bluish white and his eyes went wide a moment before he dropped down on me. I felt heat like nothing I'd ever felt before; I wanted to say I was burning up, but I wasn't. Somehow, Roan was protecting me, or maybe it was because I was part of the Court of Crimson?

It could have lasted seconds or hours—it certainly felt like hours. When it was over and Roan pushed up, we were both able to look around and see that his room was ruined. Everything had been reduced to ash and charred chunks of furniture. "What happened?" I murmured.

Roan pushed back onto his knees so he was sitting between my legs and the rest of my ash and soot covered body. The human upbringing in me demanded I be embarrassed, but if he wasn't then I wasn't going to be either. "Cress, I—I'm so sorry," he said quietly.

"It's okay, I know that wasn't you," I assured him. I watched as he scrubbed a hand down his face. "What happened?" I asked again quietly a moment later when he didn't say anything more.

"Ariana attacked you," he said. I narrowed my eyes at him, but he didn't seem to realize that hadn't been what I was referring to.

I nodded nonetheless, the memory of a giant ball of flame aimed directly at me resurfacing. I grimaced and reached up to rub my chest absently. It hadn't felt like actual fire, but it'd been hot and heavy—like a giant steel ball had smacked me in the chest. It'd sent me flying, I knew that much. Damn. It'd hurt.

Roan blew out a long breath and ran a hand through his once again red hair before speaking. "When you hit the wall, you hit your head," he explained. "Orion brought you back to my quarters so Groffet could check you over and let you rest. When I returned to check on you, I sent Orion back to his room. I didn't intend to..." He gestured to the bed beneath us. "I never meant to fall asleep." His eyes slid downward and in a movement that was kind of awkward for a Fae prince, he frowned and tilted his head down. "I shouldn't have fallen asleep next to you," he continued.

"Roan, it's fine." I put my hands up but he wasn't done.

"No it's not." He shook his head fervently. "I—I still have nightmares—after what happened with Chesca." I swallowed. "I thought you were her. I thought you were trying to kill—or rather I thought she was."

"Well, I'm fine." I lifted one arm and slapped the nonexistent muscle. "It'll take a little more than that to kill me, believe me—people have tried." I'd intended for it to be a joke, but Roan's head whipped towards me and in a flash, his hair turned white once more.

"Who?" he demanded.

"Who—no!" I yelled when he moved to stand. "No,

I was joking. It was a joke. Calm down there, boar-man."

"I will rip their—boar-man?" The white of his hair slowly receded and he regarded me with confusion.

"Yeah," I said with a shrug. "You're acting like a wild boar—all grrrr and charging right at something."

"A wild boar?" He gaped at me as though I'd grown an extra head. "Did you just growl at me?"

"Don't tell me you don't know what a wild boar is." Roan simply continued to stare at me. Lord. Did he know nothing of the world outside of his castle? "It's an animal," I explained. *A nasty one*, I thought, recalling once when a man had brought one to donate to the abbey and the thing had gotten out. Even years later, I felt like I could still feel the boar's tusks as he'd charged straight at my backside. I'd gotten off with no more than a few scratches. Never before had I been so thankful to be such a good climber. "And it's pretty dangerous for hunters—they're impossible to tame, but lots of people kill them to eat."

"Fae do not hunt animals," he said. "We cannot eat the meat."

"You—wait, what?" I blinked up at him as he hovered a bit before slowly sitting back down.

"We can't eat animal meat," he repeated.

Huh, I thought. *Neither could I.* I'd never been able to stomach the stuff. It always made me impossibly sick. "Oh," was all I managed to say and we slipped into a quiet and somewhat tense silence after that. Neither of us seemed to have any idea what to say next.

Then, "I'm sure you'd rather ... erm ... be alone," Roan said, his shoulders stiffening as he rubbed the back of his neck and moved to stand again.

"Wait!" I reached out and grabbed ahold of his arm before he could go anywhere. "I promise you, I'm fine." He closed his eyes and inhaled, but I noticed he didn't pull his arm from my grip even though I knew he very well could with only a bit of effort. I worked at a smile, my lips twitching up. "I'm actually kinda flattered," I admitted. "I mean, you fell asleep with me. You said you don't sleep with anyone. That must mean I'm awesome, right? I'm the favorite. You fell asleep with me," I blathered on, blurting out the first thing that came to mind and somehow, it just. Kept. Going. Gods. He must have thought there was something wrong with me.

"Don't get too full of yourself, Changeling. It was bound to happen with someone eventually. I'm just glad it wasn't with a high-ranking Fae or something," Roan said, brushing me off. He hid it well, but I could tell—even my chatter was growing on him. I watched his lips twitch as he turned away. I was totally the favorite.

"And um..." I glanced down at my lap. "What about the ... erm ... naked bits?"

"I sleep naked," he said.

"Yeah, but you didn't mean to fall asleep, remember?" I pointed out.

"My pixies are under orders to undress me when I fall asleep, since I prefer to sleep naked, I assume they decided to apply that to you as well," he said. "I assure you, you were still clothed when I came back last night."

"Riiighhhhht." I pushed myself to up and rolled away to stand on my own two feet as I took in the ashes that surrounded us. At least he hadn't burned away our clothes because I was pretty sure this nakedness had happened before the whole fire and brimstone temper tantrum he'd thrown—accidentally, of course.

"It's the truth," he said.

"Uh huh. Sure it is."

"It is," he insisted, his voice dropping low as a growl filled his tone.

"Alright."

"Changeling."

"What?" I put my hands up in a movement of surrender before I realized that I was literally flashing *everything* at him—I mean, no big deal. It wasn't like he hadn't seen a woman's body before, but still ... I put my hands back down, covering my body as much as I could as I searched the room for something to put on. "I didn't say anything."

His eyes narrowed. "You are challenging my authority."

"Nope." I popped the *p* in the word as I spoke. "Not at all."

He folded his arms across his chest. "Your tone suggests otherwise."

"Hey, if you want to live in denial, that's on you," I said with a shake of my head.

"Denial?"

"Yup." Another popped *p*.

"Stop that," he hissed.

"Stop what?"

"That thing you're doing with your mouth." Roan's gaze slid down to my lips and heat began to rise to the surface of my skin.

"Okay, I'm done." I slapped a soot and ash covered hand over my mouth immediately disrupting his view. Roan blinked and then lifted his eyes back to mine. Something flashed in the depths of his gaze, something heated. Shaking his head, he turned away and after a moment, I lowered my arm.

After carefully maneuvering through various piles of debris and ash to make my way out of the destroyed bed frame, I found a shirt crumpled in the corner of the room, beneath several pieces of a destroyed trunk. The only reason it had probably survived Roan's little accident had probably been due to the fact that it was so far away and beneath something so big that had taken the brunt of the magical fire. I snatched it up and slid it on immediately. Unfortunately, however, underwear and trousers that would fit me were a little harder to come by. I headed for the bedroom door, but just before I opened it, I paused and glanced back. "I know the whole falling asleep with me thing wasn't what you planned, but it was kind of nice."

"Nice?" Roan's brows rose up in shock before

quickly lowering as his expression morphed into one of suspicion. "What do you mean?"

I shrugged. "Sleeping alone can suck," I said. "I'm used to sleeping in a room with multiple people, but it's nice to sleep next to someone too." I hadn't done it since I was really little and despite the heat I'd felt when I'd woken and the fact that I hadn't known who it was holding me, I'd liked feeling close to someone again. Sleeping with Orion had definitely ruined me. Waking up with a big muscled man all plastered against me was ... well, it was nice. "Even if you didn't mean to do it, you trusted me enough to fall asleep next to me," I said.

"And look where it got you," he snapped, gesturing to the red marks still visible on my skin.

I lifted my shoulders again. "So?"

Roan's mouth dropped open and he shook his head. "You are one strange human."

"Not a human," I said with a wink. "Changeling, remember."

After a moment, he grumbled a response. "Perhaps."

I laughed as I walked out and shut the door behind me. He might not have realized it yet, but the fact that he was able to fall asleep with me there showed that he trusted me already. *Definitely the favorite,* I thought with a smile.

CHAPTER 24
CRESS

The tap-tap of shoes on stone caught my ear and before I could get away, a familiar face rounded the corner and stopped a few feet away. Without even thinking about it, I turned suspicious eyes skyward. Okay, now the Gods were just fucking with me and it wasn't funny. This was not exactly how I'd hoped to see Ariana again—not that'd I'd really been planning to see her again, but this castle felt very small when there was definitely someone you didn't want to be around living in it. That someone being her. I'd also specifically would have preferred to not run into her again wearing nothing but a man's shirt and covered in soot and ash. Maybe it was just too much to ask of the Gods, but I'd really been hoping to wear something with a little more coverage. Like maybe metal plated armor.

Her eyes moved from me to the door I'd just exited and back again. She looked just as shocked as I was, but unlike me, she managed to recover a bit faster. "Just who I wanted to speak with," she said.

My eyebrows shot up to my hairline. "Oh?" I asked.

"Yes." She nodded. "I wanted to talk with you about my outburst earlier."

Outburst? That's what she was calling it. I resisted the urge to remind her that her little *emotional outburst* had resulted in me being knocked unconscious by a flying magic fireball. I mean, no problem—I was alive and all, but at the same time, I felt like she definitely meant to do a bit more damage than that. Emotional outburst, attempted murder—it was all the same thing, really.

Left without a response to her gross underestimation of my brush with fire magic, I managed to cough out a, "you did?"

"I did," she confirmed. "I—" She cut herself off, her face scrunching up as she tried to force the words out. I stared at her, waiting. "I apologize," she said through gritted teeth, "for my behavior. It was unacceptable."

Hell yeah, it was. Totally unacceptable. You didn't just decide you hated someone because they were different from you. You decided to hate someone because they threw a fireball at your head.

"Okay," I said anyway. "Thanks for the apology."

She tipped her head in acknowledgment of my words before she moved to the side and gestured. "I was hoping you'd walk with me," she said.

"You were?" Why did I not believe her?

"I'd like to explain my actions," she said.

Did I want to go for a walk with her? No. But what would refusing get me? Maybe letting her speak her mind would get her to back off for a while. I glanced down at my attire—or rather my lack thereof. I couldn't go traipsing around the castle looking like I'd just had a fight with a fireball, not even if I had. "Let me get washed up and changed," I said with a sigh.

She nodded. "Of course. Would you meet me at the southern wall? I think a walk outside would be lovely."

"Um ... sure. I don't know how to get there, though."

She shook her head and snapped her fingers. Almost immediately, a pixie appeared. "Not to worry," she said. "The pixies will show you the way."

And they did. I followed the pixie as it led me to the bathing chamber from before. I washed up in record time, dipping myself into the water and diving out as soon as I was clean. The pixies brought me a new change of clothes as well, and in a whisper, I promised that I'd repay them with more food later.

I stepped out of the bathing chamber with a pair of trousers and a shirt tucked into the front waistband and she was waiting. The smile on her face was forced, but at least she was trying, I guess? We didn't need to see eye-to-eye, just not snipe and try to kill each other anymore.

"Ready to go?" she chirped.

I gave her a nod and a tight smile before the two of us set off down the halls; she led the way since I had no idea how to get around the castle yet. Everything was still so new and confusing but to her, it was normal. She wove through the hallways and up and down stairs clearly with a specific destination in mind.

"So," I said eventually, "what's on the southern wall?"

"It's an incredible view," she said, "but just beneath it is this adorable little garden I thought I could show you. It's just through here."

She pushed a door open and the wind slapped me in the face. I winced but trailed behind her as we left the inside of the castle. Once we were out in it, it wasn't so bad, but the difference between inside and outside the castle was stark. When was the last time I'd been outside? My eyes widened when I realized just how high up the castle wall was. We walked along the parapet and when we rounded a corner I was struck by the sudden explosion of different shades of green and the variety of vibrant colors that seemed to come from nowhere.

"I wanted the chance to explain my position and yours," Ariana said suddenly. I frowned, turning towards her as she spoke. "You see, the problem I'm having is that Roan was promised to me by his mother. After the whole fiasco with his last fiancée, the Crimson Queen wanted to ensure that her son wouldn't choose an unsuitable partner again. Franchesca, the little fool, thought she could be the next Crimson Queen, not that Roan's mother would have ever given her seat up. She'd keep the damn thing for herself before giving it up to a child like Frannie."

Ariana sighed. *Interesting,* I thought. So, Ariana had known his last fiancée personally. "And everything was going swimmingly. Roan and I enjoyed each other physically quite frequently and with the pressure I know he's getting from his mother and the Court of Crimson, I was expecting a proposal any day."

We came to a slow stop at the top of the wall and I looked down into the castle's garden. It was beautiful, but her words were ruining the magical feeling of being in a Fae castle.

"Then, you came into the picture," she continued, her smile tightening until it looked like someone had taken a hammer and nails to her face to keep the corners of her lips tilted up. "Roan has lost sight of his potential—*again*." She paused and gave me the look. The one that was a precursor to something insulting. Why did everyone want to insult me so badly? What had I ever done? I mean, sure, I'd accidentally broken into a magical Fae castle. There was that. And okay, maybe Roan was a little bit interested in me. I was his favorite after all. And I could see how I'd be perceived as a homewrecker if he was actually interested in marrying Ariana, but from what I'd seen thus far, he wasn't. So, really, all of this insulting was just uncalled for.

As I rambled on in my head, trying to work out the logistics of insulting, Ariana had kept talking. "He's completely fascinated by you, doesn't even want me in his bed anymore, when I'm the only one that can put up with his particular ... interests." My ears perked up at that.

"Interests?" I repeated. What kind of interests was she talking about?

She nodded. "Most women prefer lovers who are more giving—less selfish and demanding." *Oh?* I thought, not sure exactly how that explained his interests. Sexual, I got that, but I'd assumed she'd meant something darker like ... well, honestly, I couldn't think of anything. "I don't care about the sex," she said suddenly, drawing my attention back to her. "I've had my sights set on him for ages, now. Roan was almost mine, too. Until you. You just waltzed in and blew up my carefully orchestrated plans. Now, we've been informed that we aren't allowed out of our rooms, the throne room is off limits to anyone who isn't a royal, and anyone who looks at Roan wrong is threatened with the iron dungeon—oh the others might've been the ones to inform the rest of the court, but I know it's from Roan. And it's all because of you."

She came to a stop at the end of her tirade and I stood there, shifting from one foot to the other. I wished I could say I was surprised by her speech, but it had been along the lines of what I had expected. Essentially, it was the 'keep your hands off my toy because it's mine and I don't share' speech. I couldn't deny that there was something between Roan and me, some kind of attraction, a pull, that seemed to make us fight our more rational sides and follow our baser instincts. When Ariana stepped closer to the edge of the wall and looked out beyond on the other side, I automatically followed. I lifted my head and turned my cheek as I gazed out over the land.

If I squinted hard enough, I could make out the top of the church at the abbey over the treetops. The twilight sun reflected off of the roof for a split second before dipping down over the mountains and sending the rest of the area into shadows. A part of me missed it. It was unexpected, but with everything that had happened to me in the past several days, I craved a piece of normalcy. And that was what the abbey represented to me. A mundane life. Normal. Boring.

"Now," Ariana said, turning to look at me as she leaned over the edge of the parapet, "I would ask you to stay away from him, but after that oh so touching 'thank you for trusting me' speech you gave him, I'm sure you won't. I understand what happens when a female spends the night in Roan's room. I'm sure he showed you a good time and made that little virgin pussy of yours ache in just the right way. He can be spectacular in bed, with the right coaching, of course, and he will make a powerful husband and ruler, but I'll be the one pulling the strings from behind the throne, just like his mother did with his father. That, my dear, is the power of being a female Fae. One you will never fully get to understand, I'm afraid."

"What?" I blinked as I turned away from the trees and mountains and faced her, but it was too late. Ariana lifted her hand, palm outward and my eyes widened as a fireball erupted from her fingertips and slammed into me in much the same way it had before. Unlike last time, however, there was no wall at my back.

Instead, I was sent flying outward and right over the parapet. The wind that surrounded the fire was what hit me first, right in the face, knocking my head back just as the back of my knees hit the lower wall. I grabbed and clawed with my hands as I went over and tried to find something to grab onto, sure that if I let myself fall, it would be to my death. From this height, there was no doubt that's what it would be, but I found nothing except smooth stone. As I fell, a shrill scream was ripped from my throat.

Ariana's face was the last thing I saw, peeking out over the edge of the wall as I fell down, down, down into nothing but darkness.

CHAPTER 25
CRESS

Ariana's face couldn't be the last thing I saw before I died, I thought. *That just wasn't right.* I didn't want her face to be the last thing imprinted in my mind, so as I fell, I squeezed my eyes shut and tried to think of anything else. Surprisingly, Orion's face appeared. Even falling to my death as I was—seeing his dark eyes, gazing at me with such sincerity made my skin heat. I captured that image and held it close, squeezing it tightly even as another image popped up next to it. Of Roan. I was reaching for his image just as the ground rushed up to greet me and strangely, a wave of wind swept up under my body—slowing my descent for a split second and nearly bringing me to a stop hovering over nothing. But then it disappeared, and I landed.

When my back slammed into the ground, it felt like every bone in my body broke, organs were shredded. It hurt. Gods, it fucking hurt. This was it. This was the end. The agony. The pain. Oh, the humanity! The sheer torture whipped through me and ... *actually,* I pulled up short a moment later. I'd really expected that falling from the top of a castle would hurt a bit more than this. I cracked open one eye and peered around. There was no mistaking it, I'd definitely landed from a great height, the tall mountain of a castle towered over me. Ariana had disappeared too. So, why the fuck wasn't I a broken, bleeding mess? Oh, scratch that, I was bleeding—but my legs and arms weren't broken. Nothing was shattered. It was ... odd.

I hesitated to get up, sure that my mind just hadn't caught up with what happened to me. After several moments of just lying there, my back against the cold ground, I decided to just chance it. I leveraged up and found a nearby trunk to help me stand. My legs were shaky and there were going to be bruises, but I was alive. More than alive, my skull wasn't cracked open like a chicken egg. It was a Gods damned miracle.

I blinked as I looked over at the castle wall and shoved away from the trunk of the tree I'd used to stand. My hands were on the cold stone of the castle's outside wall, but unlike the first time, it didn't budge. I swept my fingers up and down, side to side—still nothing. A wave of panic filled me. What would Roan and Orion think when I just didn't show up again? Would they think I'd run away? What could I do? How could I get back in?

Try as I might, I couldn't find the entrance. A branch broke in the near distance, sending me on high alert. I whirled around and backed up against the castle wall, my eyes darting left and right. As I'd been searching for a way back into the castle, the darkness had stretched further and the last sun rays from over the mountain tops faded. Left with little recourse, I hesitantly edged away from the stone wall and headed into the forest. If I couldn't get back into the castle, then I'd just have to head back to the village and think of another way.

Despite my earlier reminiscent thoughts of the abbey and normal, the farther and farther I walked from the Fae castle at my back, the heavier my body became. Exhaustion pulled at my mind, and I began to feel the little aches and pains—far below what I should've been feeling after that fall—of what I'd endured.

Halfway through the woods, my foot slipped and I went down—careening into a dark and dank hole. I twisted and reached back, scrambling to find anything. Unlike my last fall, however, there was no wind to stop me. My ankle twisted, screaming in sharp discomfort as I fought for purchase, finding nothing but roots and dirt. It was only a moment before what little hold I'd managed to obtain was ripped from my grasp. Something swung out, appearing in my peripheral just a moment before my temple collided with a hardened root—more like a branch—sticking straight out of the hole's inner wall. Lights exploded behind my eyes and as I slid further into the ground, darkness swallowed me whole.

COURT OF CRIMSON

∽

THERE WAS nothing but darkness for a long time, so long that I thought I might be going insane. It felt like some part of me had just reached up and pulled me back into the darkness with it, and now I was stuck, hiding—from myself—which was the strangest part. I needed to wake up, so when I heard voices I followed the sound joyfully.

The joy was short lived.

The voice was one I recognized, one I had never wanted to hear again.

Sister Madeline.

The next voice gave me a modicum of relief though. Nellie was clearly worried about me. As she spoke, I felt like I was swimming to the surface and gathered from their conversation that I'd been found by some sheep, no joke, and their shepherds. One of them recognized me as belonging to the convent so they returned me there. Fan-freaking-tastic.

I supposed it was better than being unconscious on a hillside, but this was about as far away from the castle as I could get and still be within walking distance. I needed to get back and hope that I could find a way back in before Ariana convinced the guys that I had run away or something.

"I'll sit with her, Sister Madeline, and make sure she doesn't roam the grounds. She'll listen to me, you know that," Nellie said.

"Fine, but I don't want her corrupting any of the

new boys. Understood?" The sister's voice was sharp enough that it almost pulled me from my strange restful sleep just so I could defend Nellie and lay into Sister Madeline now that she didn't control me anymore.

"Understood, Sister," Nellie said, her voice the perfect blend of respectful and subservient.

I wasn't sure how much time had passed since I heard them talking that my eyes flickered open but I could tell it was late in the day. The sun was starting to sink below the skyline, creating great golden swaths of light that I used to chase and play in when I was a child. Much to Sister Madeline's distress.

"Nellie?" I croaked when I saw her sitting towards the end of the bed.

"Cress! Thank the Gods you're okay. I've been so worried about you," Nellie whisper-shouted.

"Don't let the sisters hear you saying that," I replied, referring to the Gods comment. They didn't like it when their charges talked about any of the Gods other than Coreliath, at least outside of educational purposes.

Nellie flashed me a smile, but before she could butt in with the thousands of questions I was sure were dancing on her tongue, I tried to push up into a sitting position, hesitated and nearly laid back down.

Her smile dropped and she rushed to my side. "Don't try and move too quickly; the shepherds said there was a lot of blood where they found you, and we don't know how long you were there, or how long you'd been unconscious. You could have some serious injuries."

"I'm sure that would make Sister Madeline jump with glee," I grumbled as I rubbed the back of my head. I could feel the crusted dry blood in my hair and was sure it made my blonde locks look just lovely. Absolutely fantastic. The desire to get clean was strong, but I wanted to use one of the bathing chambers at the castle, not one of the freezing cold buckets of water that the sisters called a shower as they poured it over you. I refused. I would rather remain disgustingly covered in old blood and dirt. I was surprised no one had tried to clean me, but as I looked down it looked like someone had at least taken a washcloth to my hands, arms, and when I reached up, my face too. Whatever remained behind would just have to be proof enough of what had happened, of what Ariana had tried to do—kill me.

"Enough of that," Nellie hissed, pulling my thoughts back to her and away from the treacherous Fae. "Where have you been? The sisters were debating on letting you stay a few days more when you got so sick, but when we woke up, you were just gone! No goodbye or anything." The hurt in her voice was there even though she was trying to hide it.

"It's a long story, Nel. One I'm not sure I have time to tell," I said quietly as I pushed to my feet and wobbled, unable to find my stability, and plunked back down on the sickbed. Nellie had risen at the same time as I did, but instead of wobbling and sitting back down she just went and stood in front of the door, the *only* door, in and out of the infirmary. When I raised my eyebrows at her she simply cocked one at me in return. I pursed my lips. Had she always been this feisty? I kind of liked it. "What's gotten into you, Nel?"

"Oh, I don't know," she replied. "My best friend up and disappeared on me. You left a gap, and I just filled it." Then her voice dropped and in a quieter tone, she said, "Just like someone will fill mine once I take my vows."

"Still think that's a bad idea," I grumbled. I looked up at her and could see the doubt written all over her face. "Tell you what, you pinky promise me you'll seriously reconsider taking your vows and I'll tell you what I've been up to."

Nellie narrowed her eyes on me. I waited. She took her pinky promises very seriously. It was not a promise she'd make lightly. So, when she stuck her pinky finger out after only a moment, I was more than a little surprised. Nellie had been more serious about taking her vows than anything else since we first met. The simple fact that she was willing to even remotely reconsider them was a huge victory for me. She didn't deserve to be locked away on a hillside with nothing and no one except the other nuns for company. She was too sweet and too kind for that, and I knew, I just knew, that they would twist her into something bitter and cruel like they were.

I watched her carefully as I extended my own pinky, waiting for her to snatch hers back when she had second thoughts, but she didn't. It seemed my being gone for as long as I had might have changed her more than I thought possible. We wrapped our pinkies around one another and shook solemnly. "Now," she said, blowing out a breath I hadn't realized she was holding, "tell me everything."

"Okay." I nodded and then swallowed roughly. "Just ... try not to freak out too much, okay?" She eyed me suspiciously, but I waited until she nodded in assurance before I continued.

Starting from the time I'd gotten so confusingly sick—the noise in my ears that had nearly left me deafened—I relayed everything that had happened and watched as her eyes got progressively wider. So wide that I was starting to worry that I was overloading her, but when I paused unsure if I should continue, she slapped my arm and ordered me to keep going. Damn. I rubbed the spot she'd hit. For a small thing, she hit surprisingly hard. I took a breath and launched back into it, telling her about the castle and the princes and the tests and the possibility that I might not be human at all. Her look of amazement morphed into one of horror and I watched, trying to hide my hurt as she leaned away from me ever so slightly. I forced myself not to reach for her even though I frowned. "I'm still me, Nellie. I'm the same person I've always been. I just ... might be a little more. Maybe. Possibly—considering I survived that fall, probably."

"Fae..." She choked out the word, fear making her voice quiet. After a moment, as the shock seemed to settle in, she inhaled and looked straight at me. "So, you're a Fae?" she asked.

"I don't know yet," I hedged. "But there's definitely a possibility."

"And you're friends with these princes?"

I winced. "To call them my friends would be ... I mean, it's not that—let's just say things are complicated between us."

She shook her head, her mouth hanging open slightly. "I can't believe this."

I blinked and shrugged. "I mean, yeah, honestly, neither can I—"

"No, I mean, I cannot believe you've never known. Fae have—Fae are magic," Nellie hissed, though not unkindly. She couldn't seem to understand how I didn't know, and I had no way of explaining it to her because I didn't understand it either. "How have you never shown any signs before now?"

I raised my hands in a defensive gesture. "I don't know," I said. "Something about going into the castle might have ... activated it? I guess?" She put a hand to her forehead, still shaking her head back and forth as if she couldn't believe what she was hearing. Were I in her shoes, I would probably react the same, but we didn't have time to debate over the possibility of me being Fae or not right now. "Listen, Nel," I said, leaning forward and capturing her hand, thankful when she didn't immediately tug away, "I need to get back. I need to tell them what happened and prove to them that I'm still alive before they leave without me. If I actually am Fae, then I can't stay here. I need your help. Will you let me go?" I knew if it was just up to Nellie she would, but she was thinking about the whole convent, all of the sisters, Mother Collette, even the Abbess if she ever returned.

After several tense moments, she released a breath. "Is it bad that I want to say no?" she replied.

"Wh—"

Before I could finish my question, she turned her hand over and squeezed mine back, startling me. "I missed you, Cress," she whispered, her voice choked. "I was worried and I don't want to lose you again."

I didn't know what to say. I'd missed her too—in the back of my mind, I'd wondered if she was missing me or if she was better off here. She'd always managed the sisters far better than I had and just because I didn't think she'd be happy living here for the rest of her life, didn't mean that she didn't think she could be happy here.

When I didn't respond immediately, she sighed. "I can just say I fell asleep or something, and when I woke you were gone. Not much different to the first time you disappeared," Nellie said as she smiled sadly at me. "You're right, if you actually are Fae, you can't stay here. If anyone were to find out—what with the war..."

"Will you come with me?" I asked, the question popping out before I could stop it.

"I—" Whatever Nellie's response was going to be it was interrupted by the sound of footsteps at the end of the hallway, ones that could only belong to one of the sisters. Nellie released my hand. "Lay down, pretend to be out again," Nellie whispered as she hurriedly pushed me back down onto the bed and took her seat by the door once more, pretending to read whatever book she had brought with her.

There were a few tense moments of silence where I tried to get my breathing under control so it still looked like I was asleep or unconscious. The footsteps stopped just inside the door. "Is she still unconscious?" a somewhat familiar voice inquired.

Mother Collette? She never came down to the infirmary.

"Yes, Mother," Nellie replied, her voice trembling as though she was terrified of the woman.

"Do you remember what the punishment is for lying to one of the sisters, Eleanor?" Mother Collette's voice was icy cold and I had a seriously bad feeling in my gut about what was about to happen. Nellie must have nodded because the room remained silent for a moment before the Mother continued. "Do you think the punishment is worse for lying to me?"

"Probably, Mother Collette," Nellie whispered.

"And what is the punishment for lying to one of the sisters? Do you remember?" Mother Collette asked.

"Lashes across the bottom of the feet, Mother, the quantity depending on the severity of the lie," Nellie replied dutifully.

Mother Collette's heels clicked on the stone floor of the infirmary as she stepped closer to the sickbed.

"So, if I told you that I knew Cressida is awake right now and has been filling your head with nonsense and young James was just down here and overheard the two of you speaking about a nearby Fae stronghold, you would say he was lying?" My heart nearly stopped in my chest. "A Changeling," she said, and I could sense more than see the shake of her head. Her voice dropped as she continued. "Sheltering a Fae, child? Like the ones that killed young James' parents, like the ones that killed *your* parents? I'm disappointed in you."

Nellie spluttered but didn't manage to get any kind of a response out.

"Eleanor, do you think me an imbecile?" There was an odd calmness to the Mother's voice that made me want to shiver but I shoved the feeling down, remaining still under the blanket.

"N-n-no, Mother Collette," Nellie stuttered. The sound of someone moving closer registered in my ears. It wasn't Nel, though, that much I knew.

Something sharp pricked my finger. A needle? Dagger? I wasn't sure. Mother Collette always was creative. When I didn't react, holding my breath and hoping she was just testing Nellie, the pinching sensation moved along my hand, slicing through the pad of my finger, scoring over the bones of my knuckles, and into the flesh of my palm. When she dug in deeper I couldn't stop the cry of pain that escaped me. I jerked up and yanked my arm back.

"Welcome back, Cressida," Mother Collette said

with a glare at me before turning to Nellie. "You are going to have quite the punishment, young lady."

"Mother Collette," I growled as I felt my skin heat up. Beyond Mother Collette's back, Nellie's eyes grew wide and she backed up several steps. I looked down at my hand as I stood up from the bed. The red liquid dripped along the tile as a burning sensation began to rise within me. From the wound she'd carved into my hand, a glow began to spread. My breath came in heavier pants. She whipped around and held out the dagger she'd used to cut me.

"I'm warning you, Fae. This is an iron dagger and I'm not afraid to use it," she snapped.

"You don't get to threaten my friend," I said, feeling the burn reach my eyes. I had no clue what I must've looked like, but for the first time, I felt actual power slide through my veins.

Her eyes were glued to whatever was happening just below my skin. The light from my wound was spreading up my arm. I slowly edged around the other side of the bed, feeling along the floor with my bare feet. I glanced back to Nel to see her staring wide eyed at me still. Her eyes were filled with fascination, whereas Mother Collette's were filled with horror.

Mother Collette kept the dagger out, pointed at me. I circled her, backing up and moving as subtly as I could towards the door. I met Nellie's gaze before holding out my uninjured hand. "Come with me, Nel," I said.

Nellie's lips pinched down and though there was a

moment's hesitation, where her eyes flicked to Mother Collette and back to me. "You go with her, child, and you'll be signing your death certificate," Mother Collette warned. "I've already called the local soldiers stationed in the village."

Nel didn't even blink at that statement. If anything, it made her move faster as she reached back for my hand and took it. I squeezed her and yanked her close to me as we turned and fled the room. The two of us took off, flying like birds through the familiar hallways of the convent. Unlike the castle, these twists and turns I knew like the back of my hand.

We reached the outdoors and I kept my hand on hers as I rushed towards the woods, dodging around buildings that once had felt like all I'd ever known and now felt like obstacles in our path. Once we reached the edge of the convent's land, just before we would reach the forest beyond, Nel slowed and hesitated.

I turned back to her and when I saw the look on her face—full of fear and uncertainty—I grabbed her other hand and held them both in mine, even as the wound in my palm seemed to be trying to heal itself. The power I'd released still flowed from me, my hair lifting against my shoulders despite there being no breeze. I could feel a certain call behind me, like the trees at my back were reaching for me. "Help me get to the castle," I said. "You can always turn around if you want—though I really think you should come with me." When still she hesitated, I squeezed her reassuringly. I hoped the expression on my face wasn't as panicked as I felt as warning bells began to go off in the back of my mind. Mother Collette said she'd already called the soldiers from the local village. We were out of time.

"I need someone to make sure I don't fall on my ass and crack my head open again," I said, trying for a smile and hoping I didn't fail.

Nellie snickered and then sighed. "I'm surprised you made it to the castle the first time," she muttered before pushing me towards the tree line. Relief filled me but just as we turned to go, a voice called out from behind us.

"So it's true then, a female Fae was here all along."

We froze.

I glanced over my shoulder and saw them—soldiers from the village. *They've never seen the battlefields*, I tried to remind myself. *They've probably never fought a day in their lives. After all, they've spent their time here, in the rural countryside, as far from the war zones as possible.* Still, the halberds they held made me gulp. "We can outrun them," I said quietly to Nellie. She nodded and before the soldiers could say anything more, the two of us put on a boost of speed.

Even still, the man who'd spoken before called out after us. "Don't think you can get away, pretty little Fae. It's already too late for your castle. Reinforcements have been called. It's only a matter of time before they breach the gates."

No! Horror and fear pounded through me at the same time that my bare feet slapped the cold ground. Nellie looked up at me, but we couldn't stop. I pushed her forward, faster and faster. We couldn't stop. We had to get back to the castle.

In the distance, I could see lights moving, men with torches marching through the fields that ran alongside the forest, heading in the direction of the castle. I had to get there first, and I couldn't get caught by these men or any others. That'd be easy enough ... right? Gods, I fucking hoped so.

CHAPTER 26
SORRELL

"What the fuck is going on?" Roan's voice arched over the air as he came to a standstill at my side.

"The humans have found our castle," I snapped. "Where is the Changeling?" I turned on him as Orion came to stand at his back.

"She left my room this morning, but I haven't seen her since," he admitted as he gazed out over the sea of torches that were marching towards us. With our magic, we could take them no problem, but the issue was that we hadn't been given permission to kill. I gritted my teeth in irritation. We couldn't do shit unless we'd been given our orders. There was no telling what the Crimson Queen would do to us—or even my own mother. I shuddered to think of the possibilities.

A scent of floral perfume wafted our way as Ariana appeared on the wall overlooking the front gates.

"Your Changeling is gone," she said. "She ran away, I saw her leave the castle myself."

Roan whipped around and would've taken her throat in his fist had I not stepped forward to stop him. Orion grabbed onto one arm while I, the other. "Stop," Orion said. "Not now. We have more important things to worry about."

"We should've killed her when we had the chance," I said. No doubt she'd been the one to lead the humans to our front door. This was turning out to be quite the fine mess.

Roan yanked himself away and turned, throwing the first punch. I grunted as his knuckles slammed into my cheekbone. "You bastard!"

"You're under her Gods damned spell," I growled, narrowly avoiding his next jab.

Orion's dark eyes met mine as he stepped back, and from the way he shook his head at me, I could tell that he too was as absorbed in the little Changeling as Roan was. He, at least, had an excuse. He'd fucked the girl. I knew for a fact that Roan hadn't. Otherwise, he wouldn't have been this worked up.

"Stop!" I grabbed his arm the next time he dove for me and pushed my power into his skin. Ice met fire with a hiss, and he yanked himself away from me to rub at the spot as his chest pumped up and down. He glared daggers my way.

Orion turned to Roan. "She wouldn't leave," he said.

"How can you know that?" I scoffed.

"She did," Ariana piped up again. "I saw it myself. She left this morning." Her face turned towards Roan and she sidled closer. "I've been trying to find you all day. When I went to your room earlier, you weren't there." I narrowed my gaze on her. From anyone else, I might believe it—in fact, a part of me already did. I hadn't trusted the girl from the very start and I still didn't, but Ariana was as serpentine as they came. She was even less trustworthy than the Changeling.

"Hmmmm." I turned back to the lights as they grew closer. Fuck, we really didn't have time to deal with this. "We need to move the castle," I announced a moment later.

Roan pulled himself away from Ariana as she attempted to plaster herself against his side. Before he could say anything, however, Orion spoke up. "It's only been days since we last moved the castle," he said. "Do you think that's wise?"

"Why wouldn't it be?" Ariana asked, once again pushing herself against Roan.

With a growl, he turned and shoved her away. "Go back to your chambers," he snapped. "I still haven't forgotten what you did."

I watched her carefully as her face went red with anger. "Why do you continue to push me away, Roan?" she snapped. "Your Changeling has left you. She ran away. She led the humans straight to our castle." She stopped and gestured. "And yet, still, you defend her."

Roan's eyes lit with fire. The kind that would burn a man to ash if he lost control of it. This time it was I—

and not Roan—who made the command. "Ariana," I called, waiting until she turned her head my way, almost hopefully. She knew—as everyone did, since I hadn't made it much of a secret—that I was no fonder of the Changeling than she was. But here and now, she would not disrupt us as we were to make our next move. "If you do not heed Roan's orders, then I'll have no other recourse but to have you shackled in iron and thrown in the dungeon."

Her eyes widened and she backed up a step. She knew I would. I had no compunction about punishing those who disobeyed. Despite Orion's looks and Roan's hotheadedness, they were far more lenient than I in such matters. When one was raised as I was, they learned to command far more than respect—they learned to command the fear in others. I had no doubt as Ariana gave a shaky nod and turned, fleeing my presence, that I had such control over hers.

"Now," I said once she'd gone. "What are we to do about this?"

"We could fight," Orion said.

"That would certainly please the Queen Mothers," I said lightly. Both he and Roan flinched.

"Do we have the reserves of magic to move the castle again?" he asked.

"After your night with the Changeling, you should."

"And you?" he replied.

"I will be just fine." I always replenished my reserves immediately.

"We have to find the Changeling," Roan said.

I turned to him with a sigh. "And if what Ariana says is true? If the girl left?" I inquired. "What then?"

"Then we capture her and make her pay for her treachery," Roan replied immediately, his face darkened.

Orion reached forward and clapped him on the shoulder, leaning close as he said in a low tone, "Not everyone is Franchesca, Roan."

Roan didn't think. He jerked his shoulder out from under Orion's grasp. "I'm aware," he said through gritted teeth. I looked down over the human kingdom's countryside as the soldiers arrived. Flaming arrows were launched, swords unsheathed. To be honest, I was quite surprised by the group of militia the humans had managed to gather. Though, upon closer inspection, I realized that the majority of these soldiers weren't soldiers at all, but young men—farmers most likely—in soldier-like uniforms and chainmail. As if that would protect them from Fae magic. Insects, the lot of humans. So angry and they didn't even know why.

"If we can't kill them," I said. "Then we must move the castle."

Roan's face darkened and Orion turned to look out beyond the castle walls, ignoring the cries and jeers from below. Inside the castle, the other Court members must have realized that something wasn't right because as the humans below grew louder, I could feel the shiver of Fae power ripple through my mind and body—the ties I had, the same ties Orion and Roan had to the members of our Court.

"I agree with Roan," Orion said suddenly. "We need to find the Changeling. We cannot leave her—regardless of whether or not she's responsible for this." *By the Gods, these two—* "But," he continued, stopping me before I could say anything, "I also agree with you. We can't just let the humans overrun us and we can't kill them—not without permission."

"Then what are you suggesting?" I demanded. "We cannot sit and wait."

"Roan will go look for her," Orion replied, shocking the man in question if the way he jerked his head up and snapped it to the side to stare at Orion was anything to go by. "You and I will begin the process of infusing the Lanuaet. We'll give him as much time as possible, but—" Orion turned to Roan for the last bit, "if you can't find her, you must give it up and come help us. We can't move the castle alone."

Roan bared his teeth, obviously finding flaw with this plan, and as much as I didn't like it either—the fact that neither of us seemed pleased with it made it a decent compromise. "One hour," I said, holding up a finger. "The gates will hold for that long—"

"They can hold for longer," Roan snapped, interrupting me.

"But we can't," I said. "Orion and I will need you at the Lanuaet. An hour is pushing it. Be back before then."

Roan looked from me to Orion, and when Orion

nodded to him, he cursed—whirling about and dashing off. I watched him leave and once he was out of my sight, I closed my eyes and released a growl of frustration before shoving my fingers up through my hair. I wanted to yank the damn locks out.

"That girl is going to be the death of us," I snapped at Orion as I swung around and started off, heading straight for the Lanuaet room. If Roan was even a second later than the hour he'd been granted, I'd kill the bastard myself—after we moved this Gods forsaken castle.

CHAPTER 27
CRESS

When the sound started up, dread pooled in my stomach. This couldn't be happening. It couldn't fucking happen now. We were so close, and we'd barely escaped the last set of men. I couldn't call them soldiers, not even in my own head, because they weren't. They were just riled up farmers with pitchforks. And unfortunately, soldiers or not, if I went down now, I had no doubt I wouldn't even be dragged back to the nuns before someone tried to kill me. Humans and Fae weren't at war because they wanted to show off their battle skills. Humans and Fae *hated* each other, and I was no longer on the human side. If I died right now it would put Nellie at risk which was something I couldn't do.

I tried to block it out, focusing on the shouting of the angry mob that was closing in on the castle just as quickly as we were. While they had a nice road to travel down we were fighting brambles and prickly grasses that grew wild in the area. It reminded me of the first night when I found the castle. *What a wild way to come full circle*, I thought.

The sound in my head was increasing in intensity the closer we got to the castle. *What the fuck was it?* I winced as it pierced through my skull and nearly brought me to my knees. I stopped, my hand finding a nearby tree trunk as I panted and waited for the noise to die down. It never did, I just had to suck it up like a big girl and keep going. I forced one foot in front of the other even as I felt my mind splinter at the horrid sound. Why did it seem so much worse now—yet, I could still stand? Maybe because my Changeling side had been revealed? Or because my powers were starting to activate? Something was different and I wanted to know what.

Nellie stumbled along beside me, hissing in pain. I turned her way, prepared to haul her after me if she so much as thought about stopping and found one of the black vines from the castle's outer walls wrapped around her leg. They extended a lot further this time.

I wondered ...

Before—the first time I came across these things—they hadn't moved away until I'd bled on them, leading me to stumble into the castle and into this whole mess. As I moved my injured hand, cracking the blood that had started to dry on the skin there and opening the wound, fresh blood began to flow, and I really hoped they'd do the same thing now. I wasn't ready to leave the mess—or the princes. I was just finding out who I was and I also really didn't want to get caught by a bunch of country folk with too many sharp things at their disposal. I sucked in a breath and let my blood fall, hoping and praying ... but a girl couldn't exist on prayers to the Gods alone. She had to bleed a little first.

I held my hand over the vine and big, fat drops of blood fell onto its black surface. For a moment, I thought I was, yet again, wrong—that the vines weren't designed to detect Fae presence and stand down, but after a few tense minutes where my ears started to feel more and more like they were going to burst, the vine loosened its grip and released Nellie.

It wasn't much, but it was enough for us to keep moving and get a little closer to the castle. When another vine caught her leg I wanted to scream. Apparently, this section hadn't got the information yet. I dripped some more blood onto it and when it released her I turned to Nellie and said, "Let's go." I turned and dropped down, holding my arms out on either side.

"W-what?" she stuttered.

"We don't have time for me to keep stopping to bleed on everything," I said. "Piggyback ride time. Hop on."

"Can you even hold me?" she asked.

"Just do it," I huffed.

This time, she didn't object, which was just as well, because I would have hauled her over my shoulder like a sack of potatoes if she kept fighting me. I wasn't strong, but I was determined and stubborn. The two of us made it through what was now a field of the black vines and to the edge of the castle without stopping again. The closer we got, surprisingly, the less painful the noise became—though it remained in my head throughout. Unfortunately, my exhaustion only mounted. When I set Nellie down, I wanted to crumple to the ground and sleep for years. We didn't have time for that though. There was an alarm ringing in me, maybe it was this sound that I could still hear, I wasn't sure, but every fiber of my being was telling me I needed to be inside that castle before the sound stopped or something very bad was going to happen.

Nellie leaned against the wall and stared back the way we'd come, her eyes growing wide and full of fear. I glanced back, following the direction of her gaze. I could see them as well, but just as my eyes lit on the makeshift soldier's powering through the forest now, while their counterparts marched over the nearby fields—I saw the vines spreading out in a fan. The men began to trip, going down amidst the brush and tall grasses. They were getting stuck in the vines. Men who were trying to capture us, to harm us, possibly even kill us were being attacked by vines. Never thought I'd be so grateful for some nature. Even as the men used their torches to try and burn the vines away, it only seemed to add to the strength and size of the long animated plants. I turned back and focused on the task at hand.

I placed my hands on the wall, not knowing what else to do and took a deep breath. *Okay, time to convince a big ol' magic castle to let me in.* "Hi there," I started, earning a look of 'what the fuck' from Nellie. "Give me a break," I whispered her way before she could say anything. "I've only done this once before and it was an accident."

"Dear Gods," she whispered, smacking herself in the face, "you're going to get us both killed."

I ignored that and turned my gaze back to the big stone wall in front of me. "If you could just let us in, that would really be great." I waited a beat. When nothing happened, my breath hitched and Nel released a terrified groan. I looked back over my shoulder. A few of the men had managed to bypass the vines, hacking them away with their halberds. They were getting far too close for my peace of mind. "Alright," I said, standing up straighter as I pressed both of my palms forward against the wall. "Come on, magic wall," I entreated. "You let me in before, you can do it again. I'm a Fae. I promise I belong! Your vines know it too, that's why they let me through, isn't it?" I paused and took a breath. No one in their right mind talked to inanimate objects—but I wasn't giving up. If it made me crazy, then it made me crazy—Gods knew I hadn't exactly been sane before meeting the princes.

The ground rumbled beneath my feet and I panicked, slipping and leaving a smear of blood on the stone. I could hear cries over the top of the Castle wall. Men and horses. *There'd been horses in the castle?* I thought before shaking my head. It was a castle, of course there were horses. Probably stables too. I'd just never been given the chance to explore.

"Please," I said. "If you don't let us in then we'll die, and I'm too young to die—and Nel's too pretty to die. We'd really like to avoid that if at all possible."

Nel groaned again. "I can't believe this," she hissed.

Again, I ignored her. Her new name was now going to be Negative Nellie—I snickered internally. At the moment, it was very apt. "They're looking for me, aren't they?" I asked the castle. "I know they are, right? The longer they delay, the more damage you take from the attackers. If you won't do it for me, then do it for yourself. Besides, it wasn't even my choice to leave you, I was pushed." Still, nothing happened and I was starting to lose hope. I didn't know what the price was to get the door to open, but I hadn't hit on it yet.

My shoulders slumped and I leaned forward, pressing my forehead against the wall. "I want to be who I was born to be," I said quietly. "I want to learn what it means to be Fae, to be a member of the Court of Crimson—to be well and truly fucked by Prince Orion, to eat food I actually enjoy, and to devour all the knowledge I can in that library that Groffet cares for. Please, don't let me miss out on that. I don't want to be left behind again."

The ground beneath our feet rumbled for a second time, this time much harder. It shook as though a great wheel was turning. When a door appeared in the brick I wanted to weep with joy, but we weren't safe yet. Without even stopping to think, I turned, snatched Nellie's hand and yanked her behind me until the both of us went tumbling through the door, and into the main courtyard, which shouldn't have been possible since the courtyard would have been on the opposite side of the castle by my estimations. I looked up and eyed the castle and its walls now surrounding us. Magic castles, so temperamental.

CHAPTER 28
CRESS

I pushed to my feet and brushed some of the dirt from my clothing before noticing a streak of black and red as a certain prince sped towards the castle's front gates on a tall, ebony stallion. "Roan!" I cried as I sprinted towards him, the horse not giving a damn that I was trying to get its rider's attention. Finally, my mad dash and frantic waving must have succeeded because his eyes went as big as saucers and he jerked on the reins of the stallion, bringing the giant creature to a halt before directing it my way.

Nel coughed behind me and slowly began to get off the ground as Roan rode up, releasing the reins long enough to leverage one thick, masculine leg over his saddle and hop down. His long legs ate up the remainder of the distance between us as he stormed my way. He didn't stop when he reached me either. His arms came down on either side of me, fingers digging into my sides as he wrapped me up and lifted me until

I had to wrap my legs around his waist to keep from sliding back down. His hold tightened as he threatened to squeeze the life out of me. I couldn't help myself, I relished in the embrace. I leaned forward and stuffed my face against his throat as I inhaled his scent and tightened my arms around his shoulders. Abruptly, his arms loosened, and he pulled his head away as though he just remembered who I was and where we were. My heart deflated more than I wanted to admit when he set me back on the ground and his eyes took on a dangerous glint.

"Where were you?" he growled. "Do you have any fucking clue the mess we're in? And who is this?" He pointed at Nellie, wrinkling his nose as her scent caught on the wind. He growled again, stepping back. "A human? You brought a human here? Were you the one responsible for this?"

As Nellie reached my side, I scooted her behind me just a little so she wasn't facing the brunt of his ire. "I can explain," I said quickly. "Ariana pushed me over the castle wall. I tried to get back in, but the castle wouldn't let me. I was going to the village, but I got hurt—I think a hunter's trap. I passed out and some sheep found me. I was taken back to the convent that I came from before. This is Nellie, she's my best friend. She helped me when no one else would and I couldn't leave her behind to be punished. She knows that I'm Fae, she didn't hurt me—I had to help her. We escaped and came back here," I said, watching the expression on his face morph from anger to confusion to more anger and then to frustration.

Roan lifted a palm and ran it through his hair, some of which was literally flaming. "We don't have time to deal with this now," he snapped. His eyes moved down to my attire and he cursed. His lips parted but before he could say anything, a loud clang erupted at the front gates. Several male Fae crossed the courtyard, racing up the steps to the top of the castle walls. "The humans have made it to the gate," he said with a hiss.

"They're just farmers," Nellie piped up.

Roan's eyes darted over my shoulder. "Farmers or no, they would have killed you for helping a Fae, wouldn't they?" he growled.

She grew quiet and I frowned at him. "She helped me," I snapped, moving forward to poke him in the chest with a finger. "Be nice."

"She's human."

"I thought I was too," I replied.

Roan's eyes grew heated as I continued to glare up at him. Without any warning, his hands came up and grasped my upper arms, holding me still as his mouth came down hard on mine. I yelped even as his tongue pushed past my lips and he stole all of my anger and rational thoughts away with his mouth. His kiss swept me up and consumed me, growing more and more heated—both in temperature and in passion as his tongue twined with mine. The kiss released within me a myriad of emotions. I latched onto him just as he had me and I kissed him back.

He was demanding in his kiss, so demanding that it's all I could do not to melt into a puddle at his feet as he continued his assault on my senses. Something soft moved against my skin, the half-shredded, dirtied clothes that hung on me moving in what felt like a force of wind. Soon enough, however, everything else disappeared and all that was left was me and him.

When we finally broke away and both of us were breathing hard, Roan's eyes closed for a moment and he rested his forehead against mine as I glanced down. "Um ... Roan?" I coughed to clear my throat. "What happened to my clothes?" The torn shirt and ragged trousers that I'd put on before I'd been pushed over the castle wall—the same torn shirt and ragged trousers that had traipsed with me through the woods twice, gotten me in a hunters trap and out of the convent for a second time—had disappeared. In their place were a pair of skin tight black pants with a swish of floor length fabric around the majority of my legs even shielding the new trousers. Across my chest, a thin metal plating of armor covered my breasts over an equally tight, sleeveless shirt the same material as my new pants.

"You can't walk around the castle half naked," he replied. "I can't handle it. I wouldn't be able to keep my hands off of you and we really need to go."

"You could change my clothes like this the entire time?" I clarified.

He sighed. "It's useless energy if you can change

them yourself," he responded with a shrug as he pulled away from me almost regretfully.

"Why would you use energy to change my clothes?" I asked, surprised.

His head turned as another clanging sound ricocheted through the nearly empty courtyard. Male Fae at the tops of the castle walls were doing something—throwing fireballs with their bare hands and shouting as they tried to hold off the human horde on the other side. It almost seemed funny that so few Fae could hold off so many—albeit untrained—humans.

"Because I don't know if we'll be able to move the castle," Roan answered on a whisper. One of his hands tightened on my arm while the other released me. "Come on, we have to get to the Lanuaet. Orion will want to know you're safe—but more than that, we have to transport the castle or we're going to be overrun."

We set off at a quick pace, with Nellie running to keep up on her shorter legs. I was no giant, but I was taller than her so it was easier for me to follow after Roan. As soon as we made our way back into the castle proper, I felt like I could actually breathe again. Roan's stride didn't slow as he led us around curves and corners, twisting this way and that, only pausing once to have Nellie peel off. "Go through that door on the right just there and you'll meet Groffet. Tell him Prince Carmine sent you. You're to stay there until the castle is moved."

Without thinking, I reached out and grabbed

Nellie's arm, pulling her in for a quick hug. She hugged me back before doing as Roan commanded. Before I could truly fret about being separated from her, Roan took my hand and we were running again. The further in we went, the more I began to recognize the hallways. Within moments, we were sprinting down the long hallway that I knew led to the big ball of magic I'd seen before.

When we burst into the room my eyes darted first to Orion, who broke into a wide grin, and then to Sorrell, who looked, well, like Sorrell. Pissed, grumpy, and ice cold. He didn't exactly wear his emotions on his sleeve like the others. The dark scowl on his face only lightened slightly when Roan stepped into what I assumed was his spot and the three of them began wordlessly working their magic to get the orb to start spinning.

Strain was evident on all three of their faces, even Mr. Stoic himself. Sorrell grimaced with the effort they were putting in. A feeling, a crackle of energy as large as a storm swept through the air for a moment, but it dissipated almost as soon as it appeared. The noise I'd heard before—the horrible screeching sound that had plagued me—was now a humming. I looked around realizing that every beat of the hum matched the same moment when one of the guys pushed another wave of magic into the orb floating between them. The noise, I realized, had been coming from this room the entire time. The hum grew and faded in my mind—sometimes growing so loud that it was a scream and sometimes quieting until it was nothing more than a whisper. It remained constant even as I waited, and waited, and waited.

"We haven't recovered enough," Orion said through clenched teeth, releasing his hold on the giant ball of magical energy.

"We have no choice," Sorrell practically growled at him as he redoubled his own efforts.

"Orion's right. The castle can take a beating. We can get some of the lower ranking Fae to reinforce the ward and protections and—"

"And what do you think your mother would say about that? Not to mention mine." Sorrell released his hold on the magic with a blackened curse slipping from his lips as he wavered on his feet. The three of them stared at each other, their eyes darting to one another as sweat poured down their faces. They continued to snipe and growl at each other like caged predators awaiting their chains to be unlocked and once they did? It would all be over for the fool that got in their way.

Turns out ... I was that fool.

"What if I helped?" I asked. My question was greeted by immediate silence as the three of them turned my way. Even the cold one looked shocked. I sighed and gestured to the opening between Roan and Sorrell. "It's clear there is supposed to be a fourth person, but it's just you three. I have magic—if I didn't then I would've died when I was pushed over the side of the castle wall. Something stopped me. And my blood stopped the castle vines from hurting me. What if adding another person—another Fae—made you stronger?"

"You would do well to keep quiet and let the grownups handle this, little Changeling," Sorrell bit out. "Only royal Fae can interact with the Lanuaet's magic. A lesser Fae, as you likely are if you're even a Fae—"

"I am," I interrupted with an angry snarl.

"Regardless," he continued without blinking, "a lesser Fae would offset the balance of power and not in a good way. Now, stand back and let us do this."

I frowned at him as Orion and Roan offered me apologetic looks while they stepped back into their spots and refocused themselves and their magic onto the orb floating between them. Once again, they were back where they started—their faces strained and even pinching in pain as they poured magical energy into the ball. All around me, I felt a whistling as the castle shook and trembled. Obviously, whatever they were doing was affecting it. I inched closer to where I would need to be if I wanted to help, not that I was planning on jumping in or anything. It was just in case they asked. I snapped a look at Sorrell. He wouldn't, I knew. But if Roan or Orion even gave me half of a look of desperation, I'd jump right in. Sorrell could fuck all the way off, but those two cared and I wasn't going to let them down if I could help it.

I watched their movements carefully, seeing exactly what their hands were doing and mimicking it in my mind so I could remember it, in case I needed it in the near future. The three of them only worked for a few minutes before their handsome faces grew pale as their features contorted with strain and what could only be described as suffering. I knew I should follow their request and stay where I was unless they asked, but I couldn't shake the feeling in my heart telling me if I just took another step forward, I could do something.

My bottom lip was raw from my nervous chewing by the time I made the decision. When I stepped forward, none of them even blinked. They were all concentrating so hard on what was right in front of them that they didn't see me slip into place. I lifted my hands, stretching my fingers out as I moved in the same way they were. Whatever they were doing with their hands, I began to copy and almost immediately, I felt the orb's magic like a tidal wave sweeping through me.

Magic slammed into my chest, and it was all I could do to keep standing and moving as a gasp slipped out of my lips. The three of them jolted, their heads coming up when they finally realize what I'd done. I could ... feel the echo of the orbs magic within myself. I slowly breathed out as the weight of the magic eased a bit and instead of feeling like a pile of rocks on my chest, it began to trickle down into my limbs like water running over my body. I felt their magic, too. Ice frosting over my skin from Sorrell. Fire that sizzled in my blood from Roan. And something else, something darker creeping into my mind from Orion. It was like the four of us were all part of the same being, all thinking and feeling, but within the same body.

"We need to stop," Orion ground out. "She'll burn out all her magic."

"She wants to help so badly, then let her help," Sorrell snarled. "It's her death."

"Cress," Roan said, "stop."

"Wait..." This came from Sorrell. I darted a glance at him as his eyes widened. "It's ... working?"

"Dear Gods," Orion cursed as the magic whipped through me—through all of us, stronger than before and the castle's shaking evened out.

"Follow our movements and focus on the fields of Arenthry, that's our next destination," Roan barked.

I nodded and tried my best to follow along, but the hand gestures were more than a little complicated, and I felt sure I was messing some of them up, but the Gods awful noise had quieted and the magic ball was spinning faster with parts of it expanding outward before it changed directions and different parts extended, like it was trying to lock in some kind of coordinates. Through it all, I could feel Sorrell boring holes into me with his glare. I turned my gaze onto him instead of the spinning ball that was so captivating and met his glare with one of my own. I wished I understood why he disliked me so, but I doubted I ever would.

The magic began to burn across my palm where Mother Collette had wounded me and I hissed in pain.

The blood there was flowing freely again and not just a little either; more than had been flowing before was streaming from my palm and into the swirling vortex of the ball of magic and its coordinate setting spinning and twisting, like a red stripe across iridescent silver. My head felt light and I felt sick, but the only thing I could see was Sorrell staring at me with a sneer marring his perfect face as he seemed to get even taller.

CHAPTER 29
CRESS

My sickness only seemed to grow the more magic I used. The Lanuaet's power slid through me just as Orion's, Roan's, and Sorrell's. The ice man had been right. It was far too much for me to handle. Not that I was going to let him know that, even if my insides felt like they were heating up and my skin stretched tight across my bones, I was stubborn enough to keep going.

The castle rumbled and swayed. I kept my gaze focused on the magical orb. At least now I realized what this thing did. So much was starting to make sense that hadn't before. The noise in my head. The castle's magic. This orb—the Lanuaet thingy—was a transporter of sorts. And as I looked around the room, the Fae princes—and now I, too—were the conduits.

Across from me, Orion grunted and went down on one knee. I almost stopped the movements to go to him, but Roan barked at me to stay where I was. Sweat collected at the back of my neck and slid down my spine. I felt something wet ooze out of my left nostril. I paused just long enough to wipe it away, and my hand came away red.

"Almost there," Roan panted through tightly clenched teeth.

Orion staggered back to his feet and kept going.

Sorrell said nothing.

My head began to ache and more wetness leaked out of my nose. No one said anything, but something was very wrong. A wall of resistance met the four of us and pushed back. My eyes widened when I felt it—something like fire and ice raced up my arms and slipped beneath my flesh. I cried out at the same time that the guys grunted. They were obviously feeling the same effects of whatever that was.

"Something's not right," Sorrell finally conceded. Thank the Gods. Even if it was the ice cold asshole, at least someone had said it.

"We can't afford to stop," Roan replied.

"It's—" Just as Orion was about to offer his input a new wave of magic—one that I didn't recognize—wrapped around us. All three of them stiffened and dropped their arms, causing me to slow and do the same. I heard Roan curse as stones began to fall from the ceiling of the chamber. I looked up.

"It's crashing!" Orion yelled.

I didn't see him coming. One second, I heard the shout and the next I was being shoved down as a giant, boulder sized piece of the ceiling came crashing down right where I'd been standing. I gaped at the giant chunk of rock. *Dear Gods. That would've killed me!* I released a sigh of relief, turning towards Roan to thank him for saving me only to stop short when I realized it wasn't Roan's flaming red hair hovering over me. Instead, it was Sorrell's white-blue locks that slid across his forehead as he groaned and leveraged himself up and off me.

He laid on his back and I laid on mine, the two of us staying put as the castle finished shaking and trembling. Thankfully, no more stones or large pieces of ceiling fell overtop us as Orion and Roan rushed to our sides. Roan looked at me and when I waved him away, he nodded, going to Sorrell. Orion stopped at my side and reached for me, despite my attempt to wave him away as well.

My body felt like it'd been put through a beating. "Am I bruised?" I asked absently. "I feel bruised."

"You're not bruised," Orion answered. "But you are drained."

I groaned low in my throat as he lifted me from the ground, cradling me in his arms. I didn't even realize what I was doing until my arms were curling around his neck as I snuggled into his massive chest. Damn, he felt good against me. I pressed a kiss to his throat, earning a dry chuckle.

"What happened?" I asked. "Did we make it? Did we move the castle?"

Roan helped Sorrell to his feet just a few steps away and even as Sorrell clutched his side, he looked over at me with a scowl I didn't understand. I didn't warrant his ire so I had no idea why he was being such a butthead. "Something interfered," he growled. "You should've never tried to help. Now, we have absolutely no idea where we've fucking landed."

I arched away from Orion, nearly spilling out of his arms as I moved to smack the horse shit out of him. How dare he? "All I wanted to do was help!" I snapped as Orion dropped my legs, but wrapped his arms around my middle to keep me from reaching Sorrell.

"It's a miracle she survived," Roan said absently as he moved towards one of the small slitted windows that circled the room.

"You're a disaster waiting to happen," Sorrell accused.

"At least I'm not a bitter Fae with his head shoved up his ass!"

"Okay, that's enough," Orion said, wrestling me back as I tried to get out of his hold once more.

"No!" I snapped. "It's not enough. I don't know what your problem with me is, but I've never done anything to you."

"No?" Sorrell's cool blue eyes narrowed on me as he strode straight up to me. Orion lowered his head and glared at his fellow prince over my shoulder.

"Sorrell," he said, his voice low and calm, but still resonating with warning.

Sorrell ignored him. "You, little Changeling—" he began, leaning into my space. I squirmed and wiggled and stood on my tiptoes on the tops of Orion's boots so

I could be as close to eye level with him as possible. "—are nothing but a giant pain in my—"

"Guys!" Roan's sharp bark had the three of us turning our heads to him as he stumbled away from the window with a sick, pale look on his face, made worse by the fact that I was sure whatever power he'd fed to the Lanuaet had left him already feeling low.

Sorrell and Orion both immediately snapped to attention. "What is it?" Sorrell asked, striding over to him.

"I know where we are," he said. "We're in Alfheim."

Orion's arms grew slack around my middle and I stepped off of the tops of his boots, removing his limbs completely from me as I turned to look up at his face. "What is it?" I asked. "What's Alfheim?"

He didn't respond for a moment, staring across the room at Sorrell as he, too, looked out of the slit of a window and cursed. Finally, when I shook his arm and repeated the question, he met my gaze. "Alfheim is the realm of the Fae," he said, his voice so quiet it was nearly a whisper.

"Oh." I turned back to the other two. "Isn't that a good thing?" I asked. "We're in the country of the Fae." I'd never known what it was called—the nuns had taught us nothing of the Fae except that they were bad and evil and we were at war with them.

"We weren't targeting the Fae realm," Roan said, explaining as he and Sorrell headed back to us. He took my arm and steered me to look through one of the other nearby windows. I squinted and leaned into the frame. The window itself wasn't even as wide as my body. Over the castle walls beyond, I saw what looked to be another castle—this one coated in a layer of white.

"Then how'd we get here?" I asked absently as Orion looked out over my head.

No one answered for a moment and when curiosity got the best of me, I turned, pushing Orion back slightly as I brushed by him and flipped back around to eye the three of them. Each of them looked as though they were men about to face the gallows. A pit formed in my gut.

"What?" I asked. "What is it?"

"There's only one way we could've been pulled to Alfheim so soon—especially in the midst of a human assault," Roan answered me, his eyes darkening. "And that's if someone else pulled us here."

"Okay…" Still, I waited for someone to explain what the hell was going on. What did this all mean? I thought it was a good thing that we'd somehow landed in the Fae realm, but from the looks on their faces, it seemed more like we'd signed our death warrants. "Who could do that?" I finally asked.

This time, Sorrell didn't waste a moment before answering. He lifted his hands and ice began to form around his wrists, sinking deep beneath his flesh until drawings and artwork in blue began to rise up and mark his skin. I gaped, wide-eyed, as a crown of ice formed around his head.

He sighed before sending me a withering glare.

"There's only one Court currently residing in Alfheim, Changeling. My Court—the Court of Frost."

I bit my lip and waited. When the three of them only stared at me like I was expected to know what that meant, I shrugged. "And that means...? What does that mean exactly?"

Sorrell glared at me. Nothing new there. It was Roan who spoke up. "Cress." I turned my gaze his way, noting that he too looked concerned, both dark red brows drawn down over his eyes and his lips pinched and frowning.

"What?" *What was so bad? If I was a Changeling, if I was Fae, then I had nothing to worry about being in the Court of Frost, right?* "Are they like ... cannibals or something here? Because I draw the line at eating people."

"Cress, this is serious." Roan reached forward and grabbed my arms, startling me as he met my eyes and held them. "The Court of Frost isn't necessarily dangerous, they're just incredibly prejudiced. We're somewhat tolerant—"

I snorted, earning another scalding glare from Sorrell. Tolerant, my ass. But I didn't say anything and nodded to let Roan know he could continue.

"Cress, you brought your friend here. Your *human* friend," he said with emphasis. My mouth dropped open, but as my mind began clicking things together, he kept going. "There has never been a human in Alfheim before."

"At least, not any that lived to tell the tale," Sorrell commented.

My eyes darted from Roan to Orion. Orion frowned, appearing somewhat confused, and I realized that they hadn't known about Nellie. Only Roan had met her because he'd been the one to find us first when we'd managed to break back into the castle.

"I say let the human rot," Sorrell said after a beat of silence.

I ripped myself away from Roan and turned on Sorrell so fast my hair whipped into my face and slapped my cheek. "No!" I snapped, jabbing him in the chest with my finger. "No one touches her." The tip of my finger grew blue the longer I held it to Sorrell's chest. He narrowed his eyes on me.

"You shouldn't have brought her here," he stated.

Even if that was true... "Where else was she going to go?" I asked. "She saved me." I pressed my free hand to my chest. "A Fae like you. If she'd gone back, she would have been as good as dead. A traitor to her own species."

Sorrell took a step forward, pressing me back as my finger fell away from his chest. Almost immediately, warmth refilled the digit and it throbbed in response. "Do you know what happens to humans in Alfheim, Changeling?" he asked. "Do you know what the Frost Queen will do to someone like your friend?"

I didn't know if he wanted an answer, but I gave him one anyway, shaking my head.

"Good," he said quietly, leaning closer as his icy breath washed over my face. "If you knew, there's no way you'd be able to go with us."

"G-go with you?" I stuttered.

"We cannot allow the Queens to come here," he said by way of answer, standing up straighter and backing away. He turned to Roan and Orion. "Get ready to ride," he said before turning and striding out.

I turned my head, feeling numb until I met Roan and Orion's gazes. "W-what happens to humans in Alfheim?" I asked hesitantly.

Roan looked down, but Orion met my gaze. His swirled with darkness, shadows, and something sinister. A shiver chased down my spine and even before he opened his mouth, I knew what he was going to say. His lips parted and he uttered the words, confirming my worst fear for Nellie.

"They die."

About Lucinda Dark

Lucinda Dark, also known as USA Today Bestselling Author, Lucy Smoke, for her contemporary novels, has a master's degree in English and is a self-proclaimed creative chihuahua. She enjoys feeding her wanderlust, cover addiction, as well as her face. When she's not on a never-ending quest to find the perfect milkshake, she lives and works in the southern United States with her beloved fur-baby, Hiro, and her family and friends.

Want to be kept up to date? Think about joining the author's group or signing up for their newsletter below.

Website: www.lucysmoke.com
Facebook Group: Reader Mafia
Newsletter: www.lucysmoke.com/subscribe

ALSO BY LUCINDA DARK

Fantasy Series:

Awakened Fates Series

Crown of Blood and Glass

Dawn of Fate and Valor

TBD

Twisted Fae Series (completed)

Court of Crimson

Court of Frost

Court of Midnight

Barbie: The Vampire Hunter Series (completed)

Rest in Pieces

Dead Girl Walking

Ashes to Ashes

Dark Maji Series (completed)

Fortune Favors the Cruel

Blessed Be the Wicked

Twisted is the Crown

For King and Corruption

Long Live the Soulless

Nerys Newblood Series (completed)

Daimon

Necrosis

Resurrection

Sky Cities Series (Dystopian)

Heart of Tartarus

Shadow of Deception

Sword of Damage

Dogs of War (Coming Soon)

Contemporary Series: Lucy Smoke

Gods of Hazelwood: Icarus Duet (completed)

Burn With Me

Fall With Me

Sick Boys Series (completed)

Forbidden Deviant Games (prequel)

Pretty Little Savage

Stone Cold Queen

Natural Born Killers

Wicked Dark Heathens

Bloody Cruel Psycho

Bloody Cruel Monster

Vengeful Rotten Casualties

Iris Boys Series (completed)

Now or Never

Power & Choice

Leap of Faith

Cross my Heart

Forever & Always

Iris Boys Series Boxset

The *Break* Series (completed)

Break Volume 1

Break Volume 2

Break Series Collection

Contemporary Standalones:

Poisoned Paradise

Expressionate

Wild Hearts

Criminal Underground Series (Shared Universe Standalones)

Sweet Possession

Scarlett Thief

About Helen Scott

Helen Scott is a USA Today Bestselling Author of paranormal romance and reverse harem romance who lives in the Chicago area with her wonderful husband and furry, four-legged kids. She spends way too much time with her nose in a book and isn't sorry about it. When not reading or writing, Helen can be found absorbed in one video game or another or crocheting her heart out.

Website
Facebook Group
Newsletter

Also by Helen Scott

Legends Unleashed

(Cowritten with Lacey Carter Anderson)

Don't Say My Name – Coming Soon

The Wild Hunt

Daughter of the Hunt

Challenger of the Hunt – Coming Soon

The Hollow

(Cowritten with Ellabee Andrews)

Survival

Seduction

Surrender – Coming Soon

Salsang Chronicles

(cowritten with Serena Akeroyd)

Stained Egos

Stained Hearts

Stained Minds

Stained Bonds

Stained Souls

Salsang Chronicles Box Set

Cerberus

Daughter of Persephone

Daughter of Hades

Queen of the Underworld

Cerberus Box Set

Hera's Gift (A Cerberus Series Novella)

Four Worlds

Wounding Atlantis

Finding Hyperborea

Escaping El Dorado

Embracing Agartha – Coming Soon

Wardens of Midnight

Woman of Midnight (A Wardens of Midnight Novella)

Sanctuary at Midnight

The Siren Legacy

The Oracle (A Siren Legacy Novella)

The Siren's Son

The Siren's Eyes

The Siren's Code

The Siren's Heart

The Banshee (A Siren Legacy Novella)

The Siren's Bride

Fury's Valentine (A Siren Legacy Novella)

Made in United States
Orlando, FL
21 July 2023